CH00850614

Born in Margate, Michelle Lloyd attended a grammar school at Broadstairs and, in spite of a rare and crippling physical condition, is now studying English, American Literature and creative writing at university. The first book in this series, *Timothy Bloom's Supernatural Adventure*, was published in 2004. *The Second Chance: A School At Elder Wood* followed in 2010. This is the last book of the trilogy.

By the same author:
Timothy Bloom's Supernatural Adventure
The Second Chance: A School At Elder Wood

EASY RIDGE:
A School with a Difference

Michelle Lloyd

Con-Psy Publications

First published in Great Britain in 2010 by
CON-PSY PUBLICATIONS
P.O. BOX 14
GREENFORD
MIDDLESEX, UB6 OUR

Copyright © Michelle Lloyd 2010
The right of Michelle Lloyd to be identified as the author of this work
has been asserted by her in accordance with the Copyright, Designs
and Patents Act 1988.

All rights reserved. No part of this publication may be reproduced,
transmitted, or stored in a retrieval system, in any form or by any
means, without permission in writing from the publisher, nor be
otherwise circulated in any form of binding or cover other than that in
which it is published and without a similar condition being imposed
on the subsequent purchaser.

All characters in this publication are fictitious and any resemblance
to real people, alive or dead, is purely coincidental.

A catalogue record for this book is available from
The British Library

ISBN 978 1 898680 53 6

Printed in Great Britain by Booksprint

Acknowledgements

With thanks to my parents, family and friends. With special thanks to Gorgi and Bruno, my cousin's two dogs; Alsatian and Doberman respectively. Both who added wonderful inspiration for Wolfgang and Suki

Prologue

The Story so far...

Easy Ridge was a quaint and beautiful village in the heart of England's vibrant, green countryside. Everybody in Easy Ridge knew about the one place in their ancestral past; the building that had been the cause of so many nightmares and so much regret. You had to be made of stern stuff to visit such a place, of sound heart and firm bones. It was hard to believe that amongst all the gentle, calm fields and grazing cows in the sleepy rural village setting, you only had to go over the bridge, five miles in and you were at Elder Wood. It was an imposing building on an estate with a secretive and jaded past. It was a building which was once a place of anger, deep sad memories and tainted soil. It was an historical pathway to an age where time had stood still. Occasions had overshadowed the happiness which could have carved out such a different shape for Elder Wood Manor. It had been but a whisper on so many lips.

Having stood in its former depressed state, Elder Wood had waited longingly for the new residents to enter on to it's impressive tree-lined driveway. Timothy Bloom and his family had unlocked the front door of the multi-storey archaic building and taken a vast step into an adventure that they had neither expected nor imagined would involve them. Individually they had breathed a new form of energy back into the lacklustre building and brought back it's beautiful features with an intriguing mix of ghostly surprises along the way. Timothy...as for him, he stumbled upon a start to a ghostly adventure that he never ever wanted to drift away.

Timothy Bloom soon learned never to assume, but to wait and adapt to the supernatural twists instead. His newfound friends were beyond most people's belief and yet he knew that seeing was not always the most reliable way of knowing what spirit friends lay around the corner. Together Timothy and his friends helped to transform Elder Wood Manor into something they could call home.

Somehow Timothy's new friends bridged the gap between two distinct worlds. The spirits at Elder Wood were there to join hands with the future. Together children and spiritual presences helped to bring a new school into a long locked away and concealed building.

Elder Wood was no ordinary school. It was a place which linked the earthly realm with the spiritual and taught lessons that were sometimes hard to accept but always vivid and inspiring to adults and children alike. To go to school at Elder Wood was to put a foot into an exciting and captivating environment of spiritual activity and ghostly goings on.

However. the village of Easy Ridge was well aware that Elder Wood had already once been a school for boys with a far different past. Not all spirits were so happy to welcome the new start with open arms and there was more that one spirit with intentions that threatened Timothy's future with his friends at Elder Wood.

So take a deep breath, let your thoughts drift and get ready for the mystery of Elder Wood to unfold in front of your eyes.

1

Ciu

Sarah

Timothy stared at his pale looking friend not knowing exactly what to say. All other thoughts flew out of his mind as he focused on the distraught face in front of him.

"Disappeared?" That was all he could manage to stutter out.

"Gone." Christian sank down onto the bed accidentally pushing Tim's mysterious parcel to the very edge of the duvet. It was the same anonymous piece of parchment which had only moments before been so carefully placed on the covers. "I looked everywhere for her!" He exclaimed. "She has vanished into thin air."

"Louise goes walk-about all the time." Tim offered up his only idea, desperately wanting to help but knowing the crisis they were facing was of gargantuan proportions. "Maybe Sarah is playing a game?"

"No, she would not do that." He sighed; oh Sarah was the worst for getting herself into trouble but as sisters went he had never been as worried as he was now. Shuffling back the parcel dropped on to the boards with a gentle thud. "Oh golly."

Tim fell quiet wondering where Sarah could have gone, surely there weren't that many places one could venture off to. Not when you had passed through the vortex. Not when you were dead. "How did you find out?" He decided to turn his attention to the logical section of the situation, after all one of his life long mottos had always been 'When in doubt, ask as many questions as possible'. At least that way he was guaranteed some answers. Putting his best private eye face on he began solemnly, all he needed was a pad and pencil and he would fully look the part.

"Exactly when did you know she had gone?"

"My family were looking for her when I got back." His pale friend explained. "I looked everywhere in the spirit world but she has actually disappeared."

"Maybe she's hiding somewhere."

"No." Christian shook his head. His eyes were filled with worry for his missing annoying yet incredibly adorable sister. "There are not many places for her to hide in the other world."

"Look." Tim got up off the bed. Ever the optimist, he had a plan. He hoped it would console his friend. "She won't have just disappeared Chris, she'll be hiding or at the very least lost."

Christian was looking glum. Tim felt a rush of sympathy of him.

"We will find her." He patted his friend on the shoulder. "We'll find her together."

Ever since Elder Wood had been turned back into a school the children had felt the adrenalin rush around them. The excitement was felt throughout Elder

Wood. The building had been given a second chance. It had represented a new chapter in their lives and now here Sarah was, complicating the whole project.

The two boys were on a mission. They were off to find Sarah and hopefully end the terrible spate of mysteries, which had plagued the archaic family home.

Tim followed Christian up the steep creaky wooden steps. He was treading carefully in the dark trying his best not to trip over anything that could set off too loud a sound.

Christian made it to the top first and vanished through the little trap door.

"Oh great." Tim muttered to himself. Sometimes having a friend who could materialise through walls didn't seem quite so useful. He struggled with the latch before pushing the weight of the door open with his shoulder.

"Excuse me." He panted when he finally fell through to the other side, his head protruding through a mass of age-old cobwebs. "Did you forget that I'm not into walking through walls?"

"Oh." Christian who seemed to be intently studying the floor for clues shot him an apologetic look. "I did kind of."

"Well not to worry." Tim sat down on a nearby box. "I'll cope. Let's find this sister of yours."

Wolfgang padded around the ground floor with Suki following at close quarters behind him. Who would have thought having a female hound to play with would be so wonderful? He pricked up his ears as a strange noise started to emit from one of the rooms. He quietly sidled over to the open door.

"Bonjour." One of the new teachers was saying in a loud voice.

"Bonjour Madame..." The pupils replied in unison.

Wolfgang shot Suki a puzzled look. What were they doing?

Suki eased her nose through the door eager to sniff for clues; these humans had proved all too often to be strange creatures. Wolfgang guarded her as she moved, watching out for people spotting their presence.

They made a good team. Suki & Wolfgang. The dynamic dogs of Elder Wood manor.

Wolfgang swept his gaze over all the intent faces focused on their teacher. He was still getting used to the idea of seeing so many noisy children in one place. This new school sure did mean a lot of kids. A lot of pupils and a lot of new smells. Fascinating yet oddly confusing.

He looked down at Suki who was still busily sniffing before noticing that they were being watched.

A little boy in the front row was definitely making eye contact with them. Oh fiddle bones and doggy treats. He had the distinct impression that Mrs B wouldn't want them near the learning rooms. They would probably be put in the garden or even worse, dramatic look, not given any dinner.

They should probably leave now before things got too serious. The "going without dinner" thought was definitely not something to be trifled with.

He pushed Suki off; ready to leave when a voice made them freeze...

* * *

14

Timothy watched his friend glare at the floor with a very intent gaze. "What are you doing?" He had to get the question out; Christian's behaviour had started to make him curious.

"I'm feeling for Sarah's energy."

"Oh." He didn't know what feeling for someone's energy meant but he would try to help or at least make an attempt to add himself into the equation.

"What shall I do?" Tim was eager to help his friend find Sarah whatever it meant.

"Look to see if she has been here."

"She wouldn't be able to get in here would she?"

"Generally no." Chris was still searching the ground.

"But…" Tim waited, there was always a but…

"Well we are talking about Sarah here." He pulled an exasperated face. "The troublesome little sister who does whatever she pleases. She would have been able to get here if she got mixed up in a vortex."

"Oh great." Tim sighed. "So you're telling me that your little sister might be lost between the two worlds."

"Kind of."

"Oh Chris this is a bit more difficult than I thought." He got up and walked over to him. "Trying to find a lost kid in this world is tough enough but trying to find one who is lost between the two is way more tricky."

"I know." Chris whispered. "I did not want her to get mixed up in this she is too young to start travelling."

"Well she seems to have decided that she is definitely old enough and ready to follow in her brother's footsteps."

"Oh Tim." Chris shot him a terrified look. "Sarah doesn't know what going between the worlds means."

Tim could tell from the look of despair on his friend's face that Sarah was in trouble. Big trouble.

"Wolfgang."

Gulp.

"I've seen you now you terrible dog."

Wolfgang knew that voice. Suki trembled by his side as they turned round to face the wrath of Mrs. B.

Tim followed his friend back down the stairs as there had been no sign of Sarah upstairs.

"We'll go back to my room and try to think of where she would be."

"Oh I am so upset with her." Christian grumbled. "I wish she would behave. Just once I wish she could do as she is told."

Tim grinned. "Oh no sisters and behave do not go in the same sentence."

"Louise is a great sister and Meg, she behaves herself."

"You are joking Chris. Louise is a major troublemaker and Meg is too young to get into too much trouble. It's too early to tell exactly what problems she may have."

"Oh I suppose so." He pondered for a second. "I thought Sarah was settling down though, you know really turning over a new leaf."

Tim raised his eyebrows in high suspicion. Sarah did not sound like the mousy quiet type of sister who Christian obviously wished for; she sounded the complete opposite. He spoke as someone who knew.

"She was a bit upset with me going between the two worlds but I thought she would listen to what I told her."

Oh right. Tim sighed despondently. He had had too much experience with younger wayward sisters to expect too much. "If she didn't want to be left behind why didn't you just bring her?"

"Oh yes, I should have brought her in the middle of the school party." He shot Tim an exasperated look. "I wanted to bring her when things were a bit less tense. You know, so that we would have time to keep an eye on her."

"Well she's gone to a lot of trouble to travel despite you."

"I know. I know now."

They went into his bedroom with a gloomy disposition.

Wolfgang pawed up the earth with his nose to the ground. Going in the garden because you wanted to, that was one thing but being ordered out was quite something else. His rights had been violated.

Suki lay in the garden on the grass soaking up the rays, honestly a slave to the sun, a real beach babe. Wolfgang looked up for a second to see his beloved Suki looking gorgeous. He had definitely enjoyed making friends with her. She was one beautiful dog.

Whilst he watched her sleep in the sun he thought of how upset he had been to see her locked up earlier. He didn't like to think of dogs being treated that way. Cruel people shouldn't be allowed to keep animals. He had known there was something wrong with that Mrs. Dreyford woman the moment he had set eyes on her, there was something truly wrong. A familiar sense about her eyes. She was one wicked woman. He had the feeling that he had encountered someone like her before he just couldn't quite put his paw on it...

He watched whilst Suki moved her head onto the stone ground. Lately she had put on a little weight. Not that he would say anything. He was too polite. He was a gentleman among dogs, a real prince. He moved over to give her a little lick. Her swollen belly was warm from the sun.

"Wolfgang."

He looked up to see Pandora bringing Meg over. His little bundle of joy.

"Keep an eye on her I've got to go and teach." Pandora told him before placing her down and hurrying off.

Wolfgang felt very important in his guarding role of baby Meg. He loved to watch over her and protect. Nothing would hurt that baby while he was on guard.

"Dog." The blond-headed tot greeted him in her baby like way. Her vocabulary was rather limited but it didn't seem to bother Wolfgang. "Yay!"

She grinned at him in her bedazzling way before toddling over to Suki. Oh no she was going to wake her up…

Wolfgang gently gripped Meg's little dress with his teeth and pulled her back. His girlfriend Suki had needed a lot of rest lately.

"Oh." She moaned as Wolfgang pulled her off to the soft patch of grass. "No play."

"Woof." He told her firmly. Translated:
Play where you will not be hurt on the hard ground.

Meg waited for Wolfgang to let her go before she staggered unsteadily over to the flower patch.

Oh no. Wolfgang knowing what she was going to do raced forward.

He guessed that Mrs. B wouldn't want her flowers pulled out of the ground.

18

Getting up he shot Suki one last look before he trotted behind Meg to watch over her.

She was a full time job.

"What shall we do?"

"I think I should go visit my parents to see if Sarah has turned up."

Tim nodded and heard footsteps outside his room. "That's probably my mum." He quickly got into bed and pulled his covers up to his ears. He had only got out of today's lessons because his mother had thought he was not well. A cold. That was what he had said he had. Pretending to look suitably ill, he struck a half-sleepy pose.

He watched Christian disappear and coughed, trying to look the part. He looked on, as the door handle turned. With much trepidation knowing his mum would be entering he took a deep breath. His mother, the human lie detector, was renowned for knowing when her little ones were making stories up. Tim guessed that she would tell he was not unwell. Oh drat he thought as the door opened.

Charlotte loved the school; it had been like learning in a museum. Every classroom they had been in that day had been filled with a sense of excitement. Elder Wood was much more than a building. It was a beautiful physical link to the past. A reminder of a time far from that of the present day.

"Hey." Her brother shouted out in his demanding 'I'm the boss' way.

She looked up to see him walking towards her, past all the kids who were making their way outside. He was looking less Goth like recently; wearing his uniform had been a big improvement.

"Hi had a good day?" She greeted him when he finally made it to her.

"Yeah in this dump." He rolled his eyes. "Fabulouso."

"Oh great." She had soon worked out that the best way to deal with her brother's sarcastic tones was to keep up a happy manner. It annoyed him to no end and did the trick.

"This is a school remember Lotts." He explained. "A socially constructed legal way for them to keep us locked up on a daily basis."

"You are always so gloomy about everything." She sighed. "Why can't you accept there are no conspiracy theories involved. School is a good thing, it's a place for us to go to to learn."

"I know better than that Lotts." He shot her a 'you're so stupid' look. "If you want to believe their lies then that's up to you."

"I guess I'm one of those people who does bro."

She bent down to shove her stuff into her bag whilst her brother scoffed beside her. She stood up with her bag slung over her shoulder. "Ok." She told him quickly wondering for the hundredth time if one of them had been swapped at birth. "I'll see you later."

"Excuse me." He stood in front of her in prison guard stance. "What do you mean you'll see me later, dad's picking us up, he's waiting for us both."

"I've got some stuff to do." She shrugged. "I'll walk home when I'm ready."

"Who do you think you are? There is no way you would be allowed to do that." He said so strictly that she stifled a giggle. "It's not funny Lotts. Dad won't let you walk back by yourself."

Charlotte knew why he was so determined that she wouldn't. He didn't like her to do anything that he wasn't involved with. He was the older one so as far as he was concerned he should be given special priority.

"He will."

"We'll go ask him shall we?"

"Ok."

He halted for a second not knowing whether she was bluffing before storming out to the front of the building.

There were kids waiting to be picked up by mums and dads all gossiping about the first day. They were scattered on the steps and down on the gravel front court. The Blooms had done a wonderful thing for the village of Easy Ridge in reopening the school. Callum found their dad parked over by the front gates, the same iron bars that kept him locked up as a prisoner.

"You tell her she can't walk home by herself." He ordered. "Tell her now."

"I won't till I know what's going on." Their dad got out of the car and smiled calmly. "What is going on?"

"I have a few things to do Daddy." Charlotte explained in her sweetest voice. Her brother glared at her from behind their dad's back. He absolutely hated it when she did that. "I was going to walk home when I had finished."

"She can't do that dad!" Callum shouted.

"Well I would rather you didn't walk that hill alone Darling." He saw her expression and faltered. "You stay and do your things and I'll drop by and pick you up later."

"Oh great." She enthused. "You sure it won't be too much bother?"

21

"Your mother and I will be taking you both out to dinner to celebrate your first day later so I'll pick you up on our way. No bother at all."

"You won't let me get up to stuff that I don't tell you about. You always want to know everything." Her brother grumbled whilst her dad drove off. "Why does she always get to do what she wants? It's so not fair."

Tim had just drifted off to sleep. He was deeply involved in his dreams... giant sheep were chasing him about on the first floor of Elder Wood manor. Running down the corridors, he recognised the old portraits that had been saved from the fire and hung up on the lightly painted walls. The beady eyed sheep were focusing on him in a highly unnerving way and even more frighteningly, they were gaining on him, the bleating was getting louder. The subject of his strange dream was quite odd in itself but ever since his little sister had admitted her fear of the animals he had been having this recurring nightmare. It was fear transference on some weird sibling wave length. He had just avoided the grasp of the woolly flock when there was a tentative knock on his door.

"Tim."

"Leave me alone you stupid things or I'll make jumpers out of you all! I mean it, and you can stop that baaing."

"What?" The gentle voice broke his sleepy rambling. "Tim?"

"Uh yes." He sleepily blinked at the door wondering who it was. His mother had been in to see him already. Having regarded him suspiciously for a while and asking him a whole load of complex questions about

22

how he was feeling, honestly she was worse than the MI5, she finally agreed to let him rest.

The door opened slowly and to his relief it revealed a very welcome visitor.

"You don't mind me coming up here do you?" Charlotte gazed at him worriedly. "I didn't want to disturb you."

"Of course I don't. You're not disturbing me." He sat himself up and grinned.

"Um what were you talking about?" Blushing slightly she frowned. "Make jumpers out of what?"

"Sheep." He shook his head seeing the confusion on her face. "It's a long story. Let's change the subject, how was your first day?"

Charlotte lifted herself up and perched lightly on the edge of his bed smiling happily and radiating with health. "Excellent."

"I'm sorry I missed it."

"Me too." She laughed and corrected herself. "I mean I'm sorry you missed it."

"Well Lettenby was hardly going to wait for us to have our first day before he tried to get his revenge. He doesn't really go with the flow in these cases."

Charlotte blew the hair out of her eyes and nodded with enthusiasm. Lettenby certainly wasn't the type to let things go. Not without a fight.

"I saw your mum downstairs." She remembered. "She looked busy."

'Lettenby'. The name triggered some strange memory. There was something that Tim had forgotten. Vague possibilities floated into his brain as he tried to think of what he had neglected lately.

"She came up to see me." He told her quickly, all the while thinking and then suddenly he remembered the mystery parcel.

"I think she only believed I was ill because she knew how much I'd been looking forward to the opening of the school. She knew that I wouldn't have missed it unless I really had to." He tried to sound calm as he talked to Charlotte; he would have to investigate the item when she had left. There were some things you had to do alone.

"Well you'll be back at school tomorrow wont you?"

"Mmm." He nodded. "I hope Christian will have found Sarah by then."

"What do you mean?"

He explained about her spooky disappearing act. "We don't know whether she's got to our world."

"Oh poor Sarah." She sighed. "She must be so scared."

Tim snorted.

"What?"

"Well." He thought of how worried his friend was. "She should have behaved in the first place. Thanks to her Christian has searched the whole school and probably the whole of the other world."

"Yes but she's just a kid Tim. You can't be too harsh with her, it's not easy watching someone else have all the fun, she might have just wanted to check out what Christian gets up to."

"Well she shouldn't have." He snapped rather more touchily than he needed to. "She should listen to her brother."

"Ok." Charlotte shrugged looking offended.

"I'm sorry." He could see that he'd shocked her. "I know how tense Christian is and it just gets to me."

Her face softened. "You two are such good friends. I know it's hard, but I don't think you should worry, with all three of us on the case she won't be lost for too long."

Wolfgang looked down at the little messy baby. He had successfully managed to keep her from pulling out Mrs. B's flowers but he hadn't managed to keep her from getting on the muddy grass. The wriggling muddy bundle now giggled on the grass in front of him. He knew from his days as a puppy that bringing mud into the house was not a good thing to do. You got shouted at and sent outside to have a bath! He didn't want to put the baby through all that so he thought he better clean her up himself.

"I better get going." Charlotte got off the bed.

They had been talking for hours about the best way to help get Sarah back.

"You can stay for dinner if you want." Tim offered. "I'm sure mum won't mind."

"Thanks but we've got a first day family supper of our own to get through."

He wondered why he felt so disappointed that she wasn't staying for dinner but decided to forget it for the time being. Somehow he felt close to Charlotte but now was not the time to explore his feelings.

Charlotte walked over to the door and waved at him before leaving. He watched her go and flopped down on to his bed. He really liked Charlotte she was easy to talk to he guessed. He hadn't ever talked to many girls before. She understood his world. It was a world where both ghosts and people turned to him for help. It was a pressurised job. But someone had to do it.

When she had left Tim turned his attention to the whereabouts of the parcel. Looking under the bed, the first place it could have fallen, he reached across and felt the soft parchment under his fingertips. He had struck gold. Pulling it out he dropped it on to the bed and unwrapped the two men's cufflinks – LL. The letters had been initialled into the gold plate – LL. Oh wonderful. His heart sank as he realised whom the mysterious items belonged to. Surely he would not use them to come back. Quickly covering them up he shoved them back under his bed. What was that saying his father was always using? He thought for a second. 'Out of sight out of mind'. Well that was the way he was going to play this, ignore it and hope it would go away.

2

A New Start

Mrs Dreyford took control of the school easily. She exerted power over all the children and parents alike in a fluid motion. Angelica loved to tell people what to do, authority was in her blood; it was as much a part of her as the skin covering her body. She had been born to rule over people. Never one to let her family link down she walked over to her treasured album. The book of old photos that were so precious served to remind her of her respectable family. Taking a quick look, she stashed the black and white photo covered pages into their hiding place. It was a flap of covering which hid her deepest roots. The album itself was full of secrets that no one would ever find out.

Timothy arrived down in the hall for registration later that morning having had to carry his baby sister out of his room. Somehow she had managed to crawl in while he was asleep and had caused all kinds of havoc. He had awoken to a face full of mushy brown goo being offered to him rather enthusiastically by his baby sister. Sitting up he had cleaned the brown gooey mess that had once started out as a digestive. He had then blinked at his room in astonishment. His little sister had managed to pull his books off the lower shelves on to the floor. His curtain had also been half-pulled off its rail. Basically it looked like full on combat had taken place in his bedroom. Finding his bashful sleepy looking dog curled around Suki cosily at the foot of his bed, he decided that the mess had quite a bit to do with Meg's actions.

Despite his busy early morning antics Tim had been looking forward to the school running on a day-to-day basis. He was a proud member of Elder Wood. In a way he had been its founder. The person who had discovered the building's potential. How many children could claim fame to actually setting up their school? Not that many.

"Bloom Timothy." Their head teacher called out in serious tones.

"Here." He replied scowling at the woman's back as she turned her attention to the next name on the list. The woman was the only problem. There was something evil about her very essence; she was a definite drawback to the whole school.

Rushing in through the front door, he was pleased to see his friend bump straight into him. "Sorry." Charlotte hissed. "I'm really running late."

As she dropped her bag to her patent clad feet she tried to look organised. Her extremely laid back brother Callum lazily made his way in behind her glaring at everyone in his moody mode and stood near the back. Mrs Dreyford shot both siblings a disappointed look before continuing with the official duty of the register.

"What happened this morning?" Tim asked Charlotte as they finished lessons for morning break. "I thought that Mrs Dreyford was going to put you both in detention."

"So did I." Sitting outside on the front steps she peeled her banana and offered some to him. "We were really lucky to have got off so lightly. Dad's car broke down just at the bottom of the hill we had to walk the rest of the way here."

Shaking his head Tim sighed. "Honestly I thought when we got rid of Lord Lettenby we had ended this school's link to evil heads."

"I did too." The sun peeped out from behind the clouds. Biting into her fruit, she chewed and then swallowed. "Still she's not so bad. We didn't get punished for being late. That has to be a good thing."

"She probably has her reasons." Tim mumbled suspiciously; his tone was very dark. "Maybe she's planning punishments for everyone later on."

"Oh thanks!" Just the thought was putting her off her banana. "I get enough doom and gloom from my dear brother."

"Sorry."

"S'ok." Dropping the yellow skin in the bin she got to her feet. "Come on let's go before the bell goes."

"You're right." Tim walked with her. "We don't want Mrs Dreyford to catch us again."

There was another reason she was in such a hurry. Having spotted her brother at the other side of the front yard heading in her direction, she decided it best to escape while she still had the chance.

Christian was still frantically ensconced in his desperate search. However a day's work had still brought him no luck and no nearer to any answers. His ma and pa were heart broken. They blamed themselves for their young daughter's disappearance. Sobbing and fuming respectfully back in the spirit world they had tried and failed to locate anyone to be able to help.

Knowing that his friends would be finishing school soon he lounged outside the closed classroom door. All of a sudden it burst open and the pupils rushed out.

"…Tough. You going to watch Buffy tonight?"

"Setting so much homework. Who does she think we are? Seventeen year olds?"

"Yeah, my brother doesn't do as much work as me and he's doing his 'A' levels!"

Christian listened to the snippets of conversations. They made him smile, in some small way helping to take his mind off the depression of the situation he was going through. Stepping to the side he narrowly avoided having his right side walked into. Honestly this 'not being seen' stuff could be quite frustrating. Jumping out of the way as another girl headed his way looking straight through him, he decided to keep out of the dangerous path. A pen shot past his left ear at an alarming rate. The herd of children ran past, one after the other until finally Tim's blond head emerged out of the crowd. He saw his friend instantly and shot him a shy smile, one that the other children would not see. "I don't think he understands." He heard Charlotte say as she too followed Tim out. Her reaction to him was slightly more overt. Smiling widely, she didn't care who saw. She even gave him a little excited wave, one that earned her a few odd looks from her classmates. Weird girl…waving at the curtains.

Christian delightedly waved back.

"Charlotte." Tim had grabbed her hand and pulled her to the side. He was far more aware of what was socially acceptable.

"You really should put your glasses on." He shouted loud enough for people in the next class to hear. "I don't know what you think you were waving at? That's a vase not a person."

Christian frowned at him. Ok he understood that he had to say something. But did he have to be that rude?

Charlotte simply rolled her eyes. "I get the message." She whispered. "You don't have to keep shouting."

"Fine." He hissed. "But be careful next time."

When the last of the children had made their way down the stairs eager to get home, Christian walked over to them. "Any luck?" Charlotte was quick to ask.

"No." He caught her eye and found a wealth of compassion gazing back at him. "I'm sorry to say there is not."

"I'm sorry Chris." She reached forward and touched his arm. "Don't worry we'll find her."

Affording her a small smile he frowned yet again as Tim broke the contact.

"Look." He moved Charlotte's hand off his friend's shoulder sharply. "We should get out of here. Teachers are still hanging about to pack up. Let's go back to my room."

"I can't." Charlotte apologised. "Dad's ordered a taxi to pick us up because of the car thing. I really have to go. Big brother's waiting to see me home."

She hardly looked thrilled by the thought.

"That's ok." Christian understood. "I'll see you to the door."

"No I'll do it." Tim was quick to intervene and turned to Christian with a serious expression. "You better go wait in my room. I'll be back in a minute."

Standing back he watched the pair trundle down the stairs together, talking and laughing. Charlotte's glossy hair swinging against her back was the last thing he saw. He would have wanted to go with them; he would have given almost anything just for the chance but for some reason Timothy kept pushing him out.

Having had a quick chat about what had happened that day, the two boys sat together on the bedroom floor. "How was school? Christian asked, brushing a few strands of hair out of his eyes. Elder Wood's opening had supposed to be a happy time but Sarah's untimely disappearance had put pay to any celebratory ideas.

"Oh great." Tim raised his eyebrows in much relief. "You know this place is such an excellent school environment, you know now that everything's been sorted out."

"No more spooky intrusions?"

"Nope." He lied guiltily. Instinctively his back stiffened against his bed, the hiding place.

"Good." For the last few weeks Christian had taken his role of spiritual warrior very seriously. He had been the only spirit with enough experience to help battle against the evil presences at the school. It was nice to be able to retire from the position. He stretched his legs out and watched Tim pull his books out of his bag.

"You any good at Egyptian history?" He queried hopefully.

"If it was Victorian" Christian smiled, "then I would definitely be able to help. That is most completely my era!"

Louise had been feeding Meg when she felt the cool air brush against her back. The baby giggled and clapped her hands sensing that something was a foot. "Shh!" The older girl narrowed her eyes suspiciously. A few months at Elder Wood had taught her that nothing was what it seemed and to always expect the unexpected. Keeping a look out for anything slightly odd she turned around and studied the empty space as if it were a looming soldier waiting to attack.

Mmm nothing. Well nothing that she could see anyway.

"Man!" Meg cried out happily. "Man!"

"Yes." Louise turned back to her sister with a humouring smile. The toddler had started to learn the odd word recently and it was good to see her trying to talk. "Good girl."

Meg gurgled triumphantly as Louise shovelled a spoonful of mash into her sister's mouth. "Man is a word." She agreed. "Soon you'll even be making whole sentences."

Giggling, her sister grabbed a fistful of the bright orange watery sludge and threw it into space directly hitting the opposite wall. "No Meg!" Her sister sighed trying to wrestle another handful out of the baby's hand. "We eat food. We don't chuck it around, unless we're having a food fight and you're too young for those."

"No man."

"There is no man." Louise agreed. "Just you and me. So eat the rest of your food."

Baby Meg ate the next few offered mouthfuls without too much hassle. The whole while, she played with the little jewels in her podgy fingers. The treasured cufflinks were glinting in the light and catching a certain evil headmaster's eye.

"Oh everything is fine." Mrs Dreyford assured Mrs Bloom. "The school appears to be running along very smoothly. No problems as such."

"Wonderful." The other woman ran a hand down her creaseless skirt. "I'm glad to hear that. You don't know how many worries Mr Bloom and I have had about this place."

"I think I do." She explained. "Opening a school is an immense task, one filled with complications. Honestly I do admire you both. Taking all this on. You're doing an excellent job. I'm sure that the school will grow from strength to strength."

"I do hope so." Mrs Bloom peered in through the open bedroom door. "You are so organised Angelica. I wish I could drum some of that same tidiness into my children."

"Comes from a very strict upbringing." Came the rather stilted reply. "I was never allowed to have a toy out of place. There would be very dire consequences."

The directness to the woman's tone had Chloe turning around in surprise. There was something almost frightening in her voice, an element of chill factor. "Sounds quite traumatic."

Suddenly she broke into a smile. Memories pushed firmly to a black corner of her mind. Must not give the game away too soon. That would ruin absolutely everything she had worked to create. "Oh you know. Pretty average."

"Unnaturally tidy." Chloe Bloom recounted her afternoon's chat with her husband Farley later that night. "That room; there was something odd about it."

"Really?" He laughed. "And this is coming from the world's most efficient woman?"

"Be serious." She scolded. "I'm telling you there was something wrong with that room. It was like the SAS had been in there and done a full spring clean."

"What an idea!"

"I know." She tutted as the children raced round her feet in their haste to get to the kitchen. "Will you please slow down! You're both going to cause an accident."

"It's sausages for tea!" Louise shouted back by way of an explanation. "If I don't get there Tim will pick all the best ones."

"How can you pick best sausages?" Farley sounded puzzled. "They're all the same aren't they?"

"No of course not dad." Louise sighed still in hot pursuit of her brother. "I like the crispy overcooked ones and so does Tim."

"Oh I see." He clearly didn't.

"Children." Chloe smiled at her husband. "I've had years of experience with them and I still don't quite understand their peculiar little ways."

Putting an arm around his wife, he steered them both through to the archaic kitchen. Their children were noisily clamouring across the pine table, fighting for the right to fork up the best sausages. Mia Valtner, their housekeeper and general source of information was busily dishing out doles of mash potato and onion gravy.

As he took a seat next to his family, Farley realised just how lucky he was to have left the busy world of finance. Banking was not even a patch on the joy of family life. The city life had been far too chaotic and it had totally set him off kilter. Family life was very important and now was he enjoying it.

"Dad!" Louise wailed to his right making him jump as his son stuck his fork in the last sausage on the plate. "Look he's taking it."

"It's mine." Timothy was explaining patiently. "You know the rules. I pushed my fork in first."

"So what?"

"So it's mine."

"Dad!"

"Dad!"

"Ok. He cut in. "Give it to me."

Both children looked horrified.

Standing up he took the sausage cutting it in half and deposited either bit on the two plates.

"Right." He announced proudly. "Problem solved."

Back in the spirit world Christian sat glumly around a family table of his own. "Ma, I wish you would calm down."

"How?" She screeched. "How can I?"

"I know this is serious."

"Your little sister is missing." His mother was pacing the small space between the kitchen and the lounge with a baby under each arm. The twins both sensing the drama. "Sarah is so young. What if something happens to her?"

"It surely will not." Both of his young siblings were pulling and tugging at their mother's sleeve, they had picked up on the tension and were playing up. "You know Sarah, she'll be fine."

"Oh where is she?" Staring despairingly out of the window she frowned into the cloudy foggy scene. "I just wish she would come home."

Charlotte cringed as her mother produced a tray of black offerings. These delectable delights were meant to be Yorkshire puddings but they looked more like charcoal rock cakes. "Lovely." She licked her lips pretending to look enthusiastic. "They look great mum."

"Oh what!" Her brother loped in characteristically far less sensitive to their mother's emotions than his young sister. "What on earth are they meant to be?"

"Yorkshire puddings." Charlotte put in hurriedly.

"No way."

"Yes way." Their mother whacked him on the head with her dishcloth. "Now sit down and eat."

"You don't expect us to eat these do you?" Callum moaned. "You'll make us sick."

"Don't be rude." Charlotte tried to be diplomatic. "They aren't that bad."

"Oh Callum!" Their father walked in and instantly launched into tough parent mode. "What have I told you about putting those blasted weight things in the kitchen."

"They're not mine." He smirked as Charlotte tried to repair the damage.

"Then what…"

"It's our dinner." She hissed at their confused looking father.

"Oh!"

"Well it's not anymore." Their mother, having heard their conversation, turned around from the sink and whipped the controversial tray away from them. "You can all starve. I slave away for hours and this is the thanks I get. Put a hot meal in front of you all."

"Now hang on Dear." Charlotte's father looking contrite tried to appease his wife. "In fairness I could hardly have been expected to guess that it was our dinner."

Callum burst out laughing just as their mother's back stiffened.

Oh gosh this was not going well. Rising to her feet Charlotte shot her father a 'don't even go there' look. "Maybe you should take Callum out to get some pizza and I'll stay to help mum clean up."

Nodding and looking relieved he grabbed his car keys, both males in the family were quick to get away from the emotional kitchen scene.

"Now mum." She soothed whilst surreptitiously emptying the blackened tray's contents into the bin. "Really they don't mean to be so insensitive."

"I know." Her mother sniffed. "I just try so hard and they don't appreciate it."

"They do." She rubbed her mum's back. "Honestly. They just don't know how to show it."

"Thanks love." Turning she embraced her daughter in a massive soapy hug. "I don't know what I'd do without you."

Forty-five minutes later and they were all seated around the table delving into their second and third slices of pizza. Callum and his father had apologised and even brought some weird looking flowers home as a gift. Charlotte was sure they had picked them from the back garden because which florists would open at that time of night? Oh well that would be a nice surprise for her mother in the morning. A bald flower patch. She only hoped that her brother had enough sense not to have snatched the much-loved flowers from their mother's favourite range.

3

A Ghostly Host

Timothy still thrived on the sense of excitement that fizzled inside him every morning. Living and going to school at Elder Wood had been a long term dream come to fruition, one which he desperately wanted to share with as many people as possible. Hurrying down the stairs he nearly collided with his mother who, ever the early bird was walking back to the kitchen with the post in hand. "Tim." She looked at him pointedly. "What have I told you about running?"

"Sorry mum." He mumbled meekly. "I just don't want to be late."

"Well that's hardly a likely possibility." She told him wisely. "Not when you live at school. Anyway now that you are here..."

Shuffling through the post she handed him a cream envelope. "This is for you."

"Justin!" He cried happily when he read the sender's address on the back. "I haven't heard from him in ages."

Justin Nesbit had been Timothy's best friend before they had moved out to the countryside village of Easy Ridge. Months ago when he had lived in Redwood London the two boys had been inseparable; they had grown up together and knew practically every little thing about each other. Eagerly tearing open the letter, he tried to contain his eagerness. Email had been the easiest way for the two boys to communicate, especially with such a long geographical distance separating them. However a few weeks ago Justin's computer had broken down, it was something to do with his little sister Kim and her sudden interest in computer games. Honestly sisters and problems were slotted together so easily. Since then Justin and Timothy had had little to practically no contact.

"Oh wow!" He breathed as he read. "He says he's all set to come to visit, if that's still ok?" The two boys had made the arrangement some time ago and he couldn't help but feel anxious at the thought that all their plans could be ruined by his mum's refusal...

"I don't see why not." Their mother put an arm around her son gently propelling him into the kitchen for breakfast. If she didn't ensure he kept moving then his first fear of being late might be justified. "We certainly have enough room for him."

"Radical!..." Tim was exclaiming still deeply in shock. "I cannot believe that he's going to see this place for the first time. I can show him the gardens, the attic oh and Chr...the classrooms." He hastily amended. Boy that was close.

Helping Mia serve the breakfast, his mother was only half listening. Louise however had her full attention focused on her older brother. "What's happening?" She asked her eyes narrowing. "Who's coming to stay?"

"Justin." Their mother answered before Tim could get out of it. He knew what his sister finding out meant.

"Here we go", he thought miserably as he saw his sister's eyes widen. I was a sure sign that the cogs in her brain were whirring. Ideas forming...

"Awesome!" She agreed with her brother. "Not long now 'til half term. That means Kim can come too!"

"Oh fab-ulous." Tim groaned flopping at the breakfast table. "Does she really have to?"

"If Justin's coming then yes." His sister told him defiantly. "She won't want to miss out."

"And you have nothing to do with it?"

"So what if I do? You can't have all the fun."

"But Kim's a nightmare." He reasoned. "A bit like you. And when you both get together..." He pulled a face. "Total and utter meltdown."

"Oi!" She kicked him under the table. Hard! "I am not that bad."

"Remember the map?" He asked whilst rubbing his leg. The two girls had gotten into a fight about who was going to have the last jelly baby in the bag and accidentally torn their father's prize possession.

"That wasn't our fault."

"Oh really?" He raised his eyebrows at her.

"Stop fighting you two." Their mother produced a massive box of corn flakes to use as a barrier placing it in between them both. At least if they didn't look at each other it might stop the infernal bickering. "If Justin comes then his sister comes too."

"Oh mum!" Tim began.

"No." She stopped him. "It's only fair."

The decision had been made. Justin and his sister Kim were on their way to Elder Wood.

The school half term arrived in no time but for Timothy it took an absolute eternity. He had been planning exactly what he was going to do with his best friend, what he was going to show him first, what he should tell him to expect and what would impress him the most. It was all so long awaited. Ever since he had found about the spooky goings on at Elder Wood he had desperately wanted to share the experience with his best friend. Let him in on the big secret! He was fit to burst.

Standing outside the front door he caught a glimpse of Christian from inside the house. His friend shot him a bitter hurt look. Glaring at each other he watched as Christian turned his back on him and walked through the opposing wall. He could be such a pain at times. Take the last week for example. Tim had been all geed up about his friend's imminent arrival. So what if he had not been able to spend every free minute searching for Sarah? He had a life of his own. It was time Christian realised that. Feeling the familiar sickly sense of guilt creep into his stomach, he pushed it firmly away. He could not deal with that now. Oooh this was all Christian's fault. If he hadn't have made such a big deal out of this visit then everything would have been much easier. He was so selfish.

Fancy picking an argument with him. He wanted to show him off and now he had to keep up all this sulky tension.

"Are they here yet?" Louise skipped down the steps merrily. Obviously unaware of the war. "Are they?"

"No." Tim looked away from her bright face. "You can see they're not."

"Ooh get you! She chided. "What's bugging you big brother?"

42

"Nothing." He whirled away from her as she jumped up and down around him. "I'm fine."

"I thought you'd be happy about Justin coming to stay." She shrugged. "Not moody."

"I am not MOODY!" He roared at her just as the familiar car came chugging down the drive and pulled up right in front of them. Timothy who had so wanted to be calm and collected when his friend arrived found himself red faced and hopping with frustration. Little sisters and ghostly friends had a lot to answer for. Fighting to stay cool, he saw his friend sitting in the back. Face pressed to the window, Justin smiled out at him.

Mrs Bloom served tea to Justin and Kim's mother in the kitchen whilst the children reacquainted themselves. "So?" Justin had grinned when they had finally been left alone. "How are you?"

"Fine."

"Good."

"Wolfgang?"

"Busy being in love with the new head teacher's dog."

"Oh." Justin exclaimed. "Typical."

Timothy felt the conversation dry up. They had spent so long apart that now finally when they had a chance to spend some time together they were unsure of each other. He wished they could have just slipped easily back into their friendship. Kim and his sister seemed to have no problems doing just that. Unlike themselves, the two little girls were busily playing in the main hall. The girls were using the space to the best advantage.

Sighing, Tim took a look at Justin's expectant face

and felt his face fall. This wasn't how it was supposed to be at all. Half his mind was still on his recent argument with Christian, they had been so horrid to each other and Tim had said some very hurtful things. He had such expectations that the visit was going to go well that the actual outcome was something of an anti-climax.

"Are you ok?" Justin raised one eyebrow. "Only you look kinda depressed."

"I'm sorry." He sank down on to the bottom step and Justin joined him. "I just…"

"You wanted everything to be perfect." His friend guessed. "I know. I felt exactly the same."

"You did?"

"Yep." He smiled. "Don't worry. I think we are both a bit tense. It's been difficult, I've missed you."

"Me too." Being open and honest felt a hundred times better and Timothy could feel his hunched shoulders relaxing. "It's been so long."

"Feels like two hundred years."

Both boys laughed.

"This place is amazing." Justin enthused. "I'm so jealous. Being at school here must be great."

"It is." Tim perked up remembering the guided tour that he was supposed to be taking his friend on. "Wait 'til you see the library."

An hour later and the boys were busily exploring the upper floors when the girls exploded onto the landing in a noisy giggling fit. "Be quiet." Timothy told them authoritatively. "Or do you want mum to come up here?"

"No!" Both girls replied.

"Then why don't you go show Kim your room?"

He offered helpfully. "You can't get into too much trouble there."

"We hope." Justin muttered under his breath, well used to his sister's antics. She could find trouble in the most unusual places and regularly did.

"When can I see Christian?" Kim asked on cue. "I want to see him. A real ghost."

Tim shot his sister an exasperated look. What had she been saying?

"Yes well he's not around at the second." He explained patiently, noticing the look his friend was giving him. "Um you can see him when he pops up. And don't mention anything about him to the adults. You know what they were like the last time."

"I know." Louise drawled, still miffed that not one of the adults had taken her seriously when she had told them about Christian. No one apart from Aunt Pandora, who could see him for herself. "But why can't you just call him? He always comes when you want him to."

"No he doesn't." Tim replied hotly. It was exasperating knowing that all his friends and family were wanting him to do something he simply couldn't. Justin was eyeing him carefully.

"He doesn't always come." He tried to tell his friend. "Only when he can."

"We won't know unless you try." Louise implored. "Go on Tim."

Timothy knew he couldn't just call for his friend, not after the massive row they had just had. Justin stepped forward, rushing to his aid.

"Look really it's ok." He frowned at his sister's groans. "You don't have to call him Tim. We're here for a few days, we can meet him any time."

"Are you kidding?" Kim looked as if she was about

45

to hit her brother. "This is our only chance to meet a real ghost and you're ruining it."

"Kim." Justin hissed. "Stop it."

"No." Tim decided. "I'll give it a go." At least if he tried and failed then they would know that he was telling the truth.

Closing his eyes he shouted his friend's name mentally, not as loud as he was prone to because he knew he wouldn't come. When he had finished he opened his eyes to see his sister flashing him a very odd look. She knew something was wrong.

"See." He mumbled quietly, half disappointed himself by his inability to summon his friend. "I told you it wouldn't work."

"Oh really?" Louise smiled.

"Of course really." He was indignant. "He's not here is he?"

"Yes."

"What?" Whirling round he saw the faint fluttering of light as his friend's early form took shape.

Kim, all of a sudden slightly apprehensive of the situation, rushed to her brother's side. Her sudden attack of the heebie-jeebies delighted Louise to no end. Now she would have something to hold over and taunt her with for a long time to come. Justin, who was gazing into the distance, focused hard on the swirling colours with a cool assessing gaze. He was trying to look at the situation, explain it logically but he failed miserably. There just wasn't a scientific explanation for what was happening. He took hold of his sister's hand, holding it firmly. It was a strange experience for the novices.

Louise, who was used to all this by now, rushed forward to greet Christian in a warm fashion. "Hey!" She cried triumphantly when he had taken full form. "You came!"

"Of course I came." Christian caught Tim's eye and pointedly scowled in his direction. He was obviously not forgiven. "You wanted me to. He told Louise with a friendly tone. "Who are your friends?"

"Well this is Justin." She indicated the boy airily. "Tim's friend."

The two boys said a brief hello; Justin was still in too much shock to do much else. Meeting a ghost had slightly thrown him off balance.

"And this…" Louise continued, enjoying her role of hostess immensely and pulling Kim out from behind her brother's back. "Is my friend, Kimberly."

"Pleased to meet you." Christian, who could have won awards for his impeccable manners, reached out a hand to the cowering little girl. Looking and acting as if she had just been shot, she whimpered and fled back to her hiding place. All the bravado of the past few minutes just a distant memory.

"Don't be such a wimp." Louise jeered. "Kim Nesbit you come out here now."

"Lou." Tim stepped forward to lighten the atmosphere. His sister could be a little over bearing at times. "It's ok Kim. Chris is really nice."

"Kim." Justin snapping out of his own moment of bewilderment seemed to realise what they were doing and started to unclasp his little sister's firm grip from around him. Uncoiling her fingers one by one. "Come out."

Slowly but surely her little head emerged, her face almost as pale as Christian's was. "Hi." She squeaked.

"Hello." Christian replied a faint smile on his lips. "Sorry to frighten you."

"I'm not frightened." She assured him from behind Justin's back. "Really. I'm not."

"Look." Timothy changed the subject. "Is there any news on Sarah?"

"No." His friend flashed him a hurt look; in fact he was quite sure that he would not even have talked to him had it not been for the presence of other people. "None."

"Who's Sarah?" Justin asked looking between them both in wonder. Watching his friend converse with a ghost was a little bizarre but curiosity was still curiosity never the less.

Taking a deep breath Timothy prepared to launch into the whole story.

"That's terrible." Justin declared when he had heard the full account of events. "We've got to find her."

"It's not that easy." Christian informed him. "She's been gone for weeks now. I just don't know where else to look and my poor ma is..."

"Losing it big time." Louise finished off for him. "Mothers are all the same. Put them in a crisis and they worry for England."

"Exactly." Kim concluded, the double act was back in action. "That's why we need to think this through. Children are much cooler about these little disasters. We can solve this as long as we stick together."

"We need to get a group sorted." Louise took this train of thought up. "Enough people to form an HQ (missing person headquarters) and then we can start to brainstorm."

Justin who was looking gob smacked at their siblings' sudden maturity and vocal hyperbole tried to adopt a more serious expression. It wasn't that long ago he had had to pull the same frightened little girl from behind his legs. Probably about an hour actually. Now she was busily planning away talking to Christian as if she had known him a lifetime.

"Do we have any other people who could help?" He asked. "Kids who might want to fill their holiday time up with something practical?"

"Charlotte." Both Christian and Timothy announced in unison surprised at their own synchronicity.

"Right." Justin smiled at them both. "Charlotte it is."

The girls giggled. "Ooh." Louise echoed. "The lovely Charlotte."

"Stop it." Timothy warned her in the threatening tones that only a brother can use. He turned to Justin. "Charlotte's really nice, she's been a great help."

"Especially with Eagle Eyes." Christian added. "I don't think we could have beaten him a second time without her."

"Sounds like a special girl." Justin looked at Tim pointedly. "I look forward to meeting her."

That night after the family meal the children waved Mrs Nesbit off and went back into the kitchen to talk Mrs Bloom into letting them invite Charlotte over the next day.

Justin and Tim laughed until the early hours renewing their long separated friendship. Both sharing Timothy's room, they were eager to chat about all the events that they had missed of each other's lives. Appearing bleary eyed the next morning they had both severely missed out on a good few hours of well-needed sleep. Not saying a word Mrs Bloom sat them down to breakfast and decided to keep a much tighter reign on their bedtime activities that night. If she didn't want sleepwalking zombies traipsing through the house for the whole week then she would have to enforce some strict bedtime rules.

Charlotte pulled her bag out of the car and kissed her father on the cheek. "Thanks for the ride daddy."

"No problem sweetheart."

She was waving to him as she mounted the steps, all the while watching him drive off and out of the gates, before she pushed the grand door open. When her mother had received the call from Mrs Bloom the previous evening she had been ecstatic. The search for Sarah was important and something she was longing to help with.

"Hello?" She called as she ventured down the hall. It was strange to be wandering around Elder Wood in her casual jeans and shirt; she was so used to wearing her emblem-crested uniform.

The sound of laughter guided her way as she followed the sound all the way to the library. Pushing the door ajar she peeped in. Timothy's lightly golden head was clearly visible in the centre of the room where he appeared to be arm wrestling with a darker haired boy of about the same age. He had to be Justin, she guessed. Timothy had talked about him enough for the last few weeks.

"Hey." She slipped through the door and instantly attracted the attention of both boys. "Sorry to interrupt."

"Charlotte." Standing up Timothy looked ecstatic to see her, his smile reached from one ear to the other. "You're here! I'm so glad."

Standing back he indicated his new friend, pulling him forward. "You've got to meet Justin."

Walking forward she smiled sweetly at the new boy. "Hi there."

"Hey." Justin was eagerly raking over her with his eyes. "Good to finally meet you."

"Same here."

The two new friends stood back and surveyed each other with respect. The two parts of Timothy's life finally meeting. "So I expect you've heard about Sarah?" Charlotte asked as they all took a seat around the large wooden table. The scene looked far more like an official government one than the playful one the children were used to.

"Oh yes." Justin nodded. "Christian's sister. It's a real mystery."

"One that we have to solve."

Resolved to work away at the problem, the children started to retrace Sarah's last steps. "It's what all the detectives do." Justin bragged having watched enough of a few scientific police series to last him a lifetime. "Even the FBI, when they are trying to solve a missing person case, they start to look back into the individual's last movements."

"Ok." Tim agreed. "Christian left Sarah at home back on the other side."

"Right." Having secured a piece of paper, Justin started to note that down. "So the probability is she is still on the other side."

"Or lost between the two worlds?" Charlotte queried. "From what I've heard the vortex can be a complicated process and Sarah is not used to them."

"So is there any way of trying to find out if she is stuck in one of those vor...things?"

"No." Christian suddenly materialised. "No way that I know. Vortex are immense energy tunnels, so vast that no one could check one through thoroughly."

"So what do we do?"

"I've had an idea."

Charlotte, Tim and Justin followed Christian upstairs directly to the attic. The youngest girls, after much debate, had agreed to stay downstairs as a diversionary tactic.

"Are you ok?" Timothy checked as they carefully picked their way up the old steps.

"Oh yes." Charlotte nodded. "Fine."

It was nice having so many people looking after her but it wasn't really necessary.

The attic was a dusty place. It was one that hadn't seen sign of a feather duster for years. Justin led the search whilst Tim and Charlotte fell behind. Christian way ahead of them all made his way directly to the central area of the vortex. The four intrepid explorers made their way to the far corner of the attic.

"Are you all sure you want to do this?" Christian asked. "Because this is serious. A risk that you have to be sure you want to take. When you enter the vortex... well it is surely not something you should take lightly."

"We know." Charlotte spoke defiantly. Looking round at the boys she held her tone firm. "We know this is serious. We still want to help."

The expression of gratitude was clear on Christian's face. "Thanks."

Charlotte smiled.

Tim, seeming to become restless, started to pull on her hand. "Come on. Let's get this over with. I'm not happy about so many of us entering such a dangerous realm."

"It will be fine." She rolled her eyes. "Stop being such a worrier Tim."

"I'm not."

"Fine." She took a step forward. "Then let's get going."

A tense cloying sensation had befallen the children at Elder Wood that day. Having heard Christian's plan they had all felt fearful of the adventure they were about to embark on. Visiting the spectral plane was no joke.

Timothy held back at the last second. Lettenby had been surfacing in his mind for a while. The guilty secret he was keeping was now all the more important because it affected not only him but now also Charlotte and Justin. He was debating telling Christian what he knew. Maybe it had a connection to Sarah's disappearance. Although Tim thought that even Lettenby couldn't be that cruel. Lightening couldn't strike twice could it?

Tendrils of misty white fog reached out like mystical fingers. Charlotte felt an involuntary shudder work it's way down her spine. So this was it. The other world.

It was hard to take in the surroundings. Charlotte who, thanks to her family's regular holidays, was a traveller. She had never seen anyplace remotely like the one she had entered. Everything was so... different to how she imagined. Charlotte had always known she had a special talent. This certain gift which separated her from everyone else, for as far back as she could remember she had seen people that others couldn't.

Following Christian's lead she gasped as a cold hand gripped hers.

"Charlotte?"

"Yes." Spinning round she came face to face with a concerned looking Tim.

"I'm fine." She reassured him. "Really."

"Good." He regarded Christian's back thoughtfully before opening his mouth. "We should get this over with a s a p."

Charlotte had to giggle. "Oh Tim, you sound just like an army major. Lighten up."

"Yeah Tim." Justin who had been enthralled by the new place suddenly jumped up next to them. "Relax. Everything's ok."

Timothy stood there open-mouthed. His friend's lack of concern at the serious situation was difficult to understand. "You do realise that this is for real?" He asked. "I mean what we are doing is serious."

"Yes." They both chimed in unison.

Christian who had been leading the team turned round. "Right we are here." He announced in a grim tone. "We can go talk to them now."

Walking into Christian's parents' house the children felt the first pangs of trepidation. After all, for all the hints of normality, the number above the door and the red brick façade, this was still a house belonging to another realm. One which they had risked a lot to visit.

"Oh my!" Mrs Cortex had fussed when she had opened the door to them. "Children. How on earth did you get here?"

Explaining Christian had filled her in on the vortex in the Elder Wood attic, Christian's mother offered the children drinks as they all took a seat in the incredibly tiny lounge. Everything was slightly cramped and even the ceiling height had caused a few problems, especially when the children had to duck to enter or risk a bump from the oak beam above on the head.

"It is mighty easy." He had reassured her. "Though not a journey I think the others should make too often."

"Of course not." His mother had chastised. "I am not even sure this kind of visiting is allowed. I mean it might be frowned upon by you know, the elder."

Christian did know who. The professor was one of the elders of the spirit world and generally he was the one to accept or reject any trespassers on to the spirit realm. He was respected by many and feared by most. However Christian, who had actually tried to seek out his help and received it, knew better. The professor was not an unkind man, a little hard to feel at ease with. Yet he was someone with invaluable knowledge and all passing in and out of the spectral plane was very much up to him. He was a useful friend to have.

"I think the elder would want to help ma." Christian assured her. "He's quite nice when you get used to his ways." One of his ways being his exceptional habit to shout rather too loudly at anybody in the vicinity. If you had sensitive ears then you were in for a treat as the professor did have a tendency to over compensate for anyone with a soft voice. Regularly booming his point.

Flushing at the very idea of meeting with such an important man, Mrs Cortex tutted. "Well let us not draw too much attention to the fact." Twitching the curtains making sure none of her nosy neighbours were on patrol.

"You know how the folks around here like to gossip."

"I know." Christian vaguely remembered the fuss their so-called friends had made about his baby brother's crying. Sean and Connor were crawling around on the floor trying to attract as much attention as possible; they did not get visitors often. The babies were cute little copies of Christian; both had dimpled smiles and hauntingly beautiful eyes. Little Sean had already started to climb onto Charlotte's lap eager for a fuss.

"Oh you adorable boy." She started to coo much to his delight.

Christian watched as she lifted the tot onto her knees and played with him. Oh how lucky his brother was. Charlotte's dark hair brushed the top of his baby brother's head as she kissed his podgy cheek. "Ooh what a clever boy." She enthused as he made a clumsy grab for her necklace. Both Justin and Tim were sitting at the far end of the sofa. Keeping away from the messy gurgling brothers, Timothy and Christian stood back.

"Aw." Charlotte smiled as Sean blew a raspberry. All the boys rolled their eyes. Even Connor who was playing with his blocks on the floor could see through his brother's antics.

Charlotte smiled politely at Christian's mother. "I'm so sorry about Sarah."

"Aye." The red haired lady sighed sadly. "We are all of us at our wits end. That girl..." She sniffed. "I wish she would stop playing about and turn up."

Christian who had been playing with his brothers left them to stand by his mother's side. "Don't worry ma. We will find her."

"That's why we came." Charlotte took up where he left off. "To see if we could retrace her steps."

Tears started to stream down the woman's cheeks at the very thought of it. "I can not believe she could do this to us." She sobbed. "Especially after what we went through with Christian."

"It must be awful." Charlotte agreed knowing that her own mother would have a heart attack if she went missing. "I believe we will find her though."

"Thanks." Christian whispered to Charlotte as they made their way back to the vortex. They were supposed to be retracing Sarah's last movements in the spirit world.

"For what?"

"For being so helpful with my ma. She's been so worried lately and you were really kind."

"Chris." She turned to him. "You don't need to thank me."

They faced each other in the strange twilight a smile spreading over their faces. Eyes held each other's and they both felt oddly close to one another in more than a physical sense. Before he knew what he was doing Christian had reached out and taken Charlotte's hand.

Justin was telling Tim a joke as they made their way towards the tunnel that would transport them. They kept eyes peeled just in case. "What's going on?" Tim's eyes narrowed as he spotted Charlotte and Chris standing close together up ahead.

"What?" Justin asked. He strained to see what was bugging his friend so much, but all he could see was his two friends talking.

"Hey!" Tim shouted. "You two find anything?"

Charlotte, who had been gazing into Chris's eyes, jumped at the loud shout that broke into their little moment. Turning round she spotted Timothy in the distance. "Oh hi." She called. "Uh no we haven't found anything yet."

"Ok." Tim approached them shooting them both wary glances. "I suggest we carry on then Charlotte I think you should come with me and Justin you go with Christian for a while."

Justin who was midway through his joke started to protest. "But Tim… Charlotte and Chris were talking."

"Oh were they?" He looked back at them. "Well they can do that later. The most important thing now is trying to find Sarah."

Christian looked as if he was about to say something but at the last minute he changed his mind. Justin shrugged and kept on walking through the mist. Sometimes his friend was a mystery to him.

The search was a fruitless one and a journey that had exhausted them all. Charlotte, who felt like she had been walking for hours, stumbled into Tim. "Sorry." She mumbled as he steadied her.

"Don't worry." He peered into her face. "You feeling ok?"

"Mmm." She nodded. "I'm fine."

He shook his own head to get rid of the sluggish feeling that had descended upon him. "Hey." He shouted to Justin and Chris up ahead. "You two doing ok?"

"Yes." They shouted back.

Shrugging, he carried on. Maybe it was only him who had started to feel dizzy.

Charlotte tried to keep focused on the misty swirls in front of her but it was difficult. Increasing spells of giddiness washed over her as she stumbled on. An incredible sense of lethargy started to weigh her limbs down. Lifting her leg seemed such an effort. Practically straining at the movement the mere thought made her want to lie down. However, everyone else seemed to be moving on fine so she kept her worries to herself.

Two eyes watched the children's progress as they made their way through the misty fog. Oh how foolish. After so many encounters they still believed that they had the power to defeat him.

"Chris!" Sarah called desperately.

Only with the gag over her mouth it sounded more like a muffled. "Mfff."

"Shut up." He whirled on her ready to quieten her down. "You know that I am in control. I do not even know why you persist in this infernal noise, it is pointless."

Sarah knew this, but it was not really a point she liked to dwell on. After all she had the courage to go on, a courage which had seen her through many a tough time. Lord Lettenby was in for a shock.

Chris kept checking on Tim's friend. Justin was looking particularly sleepy; his eye lids were seriously drooping. It was strange. Surely it had not got that late.

"Are you ok?" He asked.

"I'm fine." Justin snapped, wondering why he kept asking. He just felt tired. He would be ok in a while. They kept walking through the fog.

Charlotte too was feeling particularly woozy. As Tim reached for under her arm to give her some extra support she pulled away. "Don't touch me." She moaned. An unreal strange feeling had crept in and she suddenly felt very defensive.

"What?" Tim asked feeling confused at her sudden jerking away.

"You heard." She replied wondering what was making her feel like this. "Stay away from me."

"Fine." The anger bubbled in him too. "You make your own way."

"I will."

Chris turned round and stared in horror watching as Charlotte and Tim started to fight. What was going on? Justin was stumbling ahead looking dazed.

"I think." He announced. "We should all stop for a while."

"Don't be stupid." Justin shouted. "We're here to do something."

"Yes." Charlotte continued looking slightly confused. "We're here to…"

Chris gawped at them. What was wrong with them all? "Find my sister." He finished off dismayed.

"Oh yes." She half smiled. "I forgot."

Tim was holding his head. "Why do I feel so dizzy?"

"Stop moaning." Charlotte groaned.

"Yeah mate." Justin sort of fell but Chris caught his arm. "We're all not feeling so bright."

"I don't feel it." Chris looked at them all. "I don't feel anything."

"Ooh." Charlotte suddenly swayed. "I've got to sit down."

Chris was stuck looking frantically at Justin first then Charlotte. Acting quickly, he steadied Justin then ran forward and caught her before she hit the ground. "Hey." He copied Tim's modern term of phrase. "Charlotte are you ok?"

"Chris." She giggled as he held her up. She really was feeling weak, hardly able to keep herself up. "You look funny."

He stared in to her eyes boy she looked dozy. Her usually bright eyes were glazed and unfocused. He could feel how warm she was. "Tim." He called worriedly. "Charlotte's not well. Help me."

Tim was in no position to help. His own head was spinning faster and faster until he had no choice but to drop to his knees. He simply groaned.

"Oh gosh." He turned back. "Please Charlotte."

"Mmm. S'okay." She nodded looking as if she was thinking or struggling too.

"You will be all right." Christian reassured her. "Everything will be ok."

"No." She looked uncomfortable her eyes half closed but trying to impart some message. "Listen... He's here."

"Who's here?" He asked gently stroking her hot cheek. The coolness of his fingers seemed to bring her round. "Charlotte talk to me."

"That man." She groaned. "Near He wants to hurt you."

"Hurt me?"

"Yes." She sighed, her eyes fluttering shut. "You be careful."

"No Charlotte!" He shook her slightly. "Don't go to sleep on me. I need you."

"Sorry." She murmured her head drooping. "Feel so sleepy. Got to sleep."

"But." He pleaded. "Charlotte you can't be sick."

He held her up. Her reply was so weak that he could hardly hear. He turned to Tim and Justin to see they were in much similar shape. Both were on their knees, Justin was half way to lying down. "Oh no." He cried. "What is happening?"

"Can't you guess?" The voice growled. "I am disappointed in you Christian. You were never the brightest spark in the school but still… you would have thought you could have guessed."

Christian spun round still holding Charlotte in his arms, she was very droopy. A wilted flower, her head resting softly on his shoulder. "What have you done?" He narrowed his eyes at his arch-enemy. "What have you done to my friends?"

"Oh just something to help keep them out of our way." His voice was loud in the echoing stillness. "We have some unfinished business left you see. Some matters that we have to resolve between ourselves."

"What?" Christian asked. "What do you want? I thought we had got rid of you."

"Oh no." The nasty eyes crinkled as he spoke. "You may have delayed my plans but you did not halt them entirely. Your fate still lies very much within my hands and that of your sister's. Well that pesky little problem will be taken care of forthwith."

"What are you talking about?" Christian asked, the anger rising in his body. This was too much. His sister was not part of any of their past. "If you have hurt Sarah I will…"

"What?" Lettenby laughed cruelly. "What will you do? Kill me? I'm afraid you already took care of that."

* * *

62

Christian was shaking with rage. "You..." He could hardly talk to him. "How can you say that? You know what you did? You hurt me and all those other children. Your evil cruel hearted actions tortured so many. Whatever happened was absolutely your own fault."

"How droll." The man with the razor sharp look took a step towards him. Instinctively Christian's fist clenched. He dragged Charlotte back with him.

"You." Lord Lettenby rasped. "My pupil is telling me what happened at my very own school. I think you will find that you are the one who caused that little tragedy. You and your moral crusade."

"Why should I have let you carry on with your horrible secrets?" Christian raged. "Let you keep hurting everyone? You're a liar, a cheat and I... I..."

"Oh do carry on." Lettenby insisted. "I'm enjoying the little speech. You're noble to say the least."

Charlotte started to say something, her words mere whispers. "No don't listen." She moaned. "He's evil. Messing with your mind..."

"Quiet!" Lettenby was over the misty ground in an instant. "Just keep quiet girl."

Christian whipped Charlotte out of his reach. The movement made her groan but there was nothing he could do. Lettenby was no person to be trifled with. "Stay away!" He cried.

"Oh how sweet." He drawled. "Protecting your little girlfriend... Do her parents know, tell me, that their precious daughter is falling in love with a ghost."

"You have no business being here." Chris tried to stay calm. If he knew that Charlotte wasn't his girlfriend but that somebody else was he was positive then she would be in danger. "I don't even know how you're free to roam about..."

"Oh really?" He smiled evilly. "Well maybe you don't know your friends as well as you think."

"What are you talking about?" He shook his head just as Charlotte started to make sounds again. His attention broken, he looked down at her pale sleeping face.

Lettenby snapped. One minute he was standing a few metres away simply talking to Christian and the next...

"Stay away!" Christian roared. "Stay away from me."

"With pleasure." He shouted back. "Just give me the girl."

"You're joking." He laughed. "Right?"

"Wrong." With one fell swoop he had secured the girl in his arms and whipped her into the air.

Chris's eyes followed in anguish as Charlotte's limp body was tossed like a piece of rubbish through the swirling mist. She landed with an almighty thump, which Chris had to look away from. His own chest was heaving with a potent mix of anger and hurt. Where was the justice? Lettenby should not be able to get away with this, not after everything he had already done. He blinked, trying to get his brain in gear and then determinedly turned back towards his friend. Charlotte needed him. Her dark hair was the only visible part of her as she lay with her back to him on the ground. It was hard to tell if she was ok but he had to at least trust that she was.

"Lettenby."

"Yes." His previous head whirled round to face his nemesis. "What is it boy? Do you want to complain about my violent tendencies?"

"No." Chris took a shuddery breath. "I know what you are."

"Oh." The cruel man lifted a bushy eyebrow in amusement. "And that is?"

"Gone." Christian only said one word. It was a syllable loaded with meaning. It was a promise.

His eyes blazing with fury he took a first step towards his destiny. Confidence shone out from him, bathing him in an eerie glow. Striding purposefully he covered the distance between Lettenby and himself in a minute. Second.

Lettenby narrowed his eyes; a look of distrust all over his face. "Boy." He croaked. "What are you planning?"

"Something which will put a conclusion to your antics. Once and for all."

"Hah!" The evil head laughed. Mocking his strength. His courage. His character. "You little oik, there is really nothing you can do."

"Want to bet?"

A malicious spark crossed Lettenby's face. Gambling had always been a particularly nasty little habit of his, one that had led to him stealing off the children and ultimately murdering to cover it up. The little comment burst open a torrent of sordid memories. "Shut up."

"Your days are so over." Chris shouted. "Why can't you accept that?"

"Because you brat." He ranted. "You ruined everything. You couldn't keep quiet. Take your punishment like a good boy."

"A good boy?" Christian could hardly steady his rage.

"Yes." The headmaster paced the small space. "Your infernal nosiness got in the way of everything. My plans, I would have been rich and all that power." His eyes gleamed at the prospect, still desperate with the desire for ultimate autonomy. "But," He broke off in a barely audible murmur. "You stopped everything. My plans went up in smoke along with my life."

"You caused it!" Christian screamed. "You killed us."

"No." He turned his oval eyes on him. 'Eagle Eyes' they used to call him at school, the pupils taunting nickname. Not that they used it often, they were too scared of the bearer of the name.

The sharp pupils focused on Chris. "I remember what happened. Exactly how you brought me down."

"Good." Chris's own eyes burned with pride. "And I will do it again."

"You…" He started to say but they were both brought to an abrupt halt by Lettenby's eagle eyes, the ones that had earned him the reputation. The eyes broadened, widened and then with slow progress he fell to the floor. Charlotte, looking dazed and still sleepy stood with her hand still raised from where she had just karate chopped the headmaster.

"Charlotte?" Chris could hardly believe his eyes.

4

Friends

The air was charged with electricity. All around Chris could hear it crackling, buzzing around his ears. The tension of the battle had no doubt disturbed the peaceful spectral world.

Soon after her save of the disaster, Charlotte started to fall to the floor. She was still feeling woozy from the drug that the evil head had infected the air with and after her earlier dramatics she started to feel the effects. Chris jolted into action and caught her before she fell on top of Lettenby. "Charlotte?" He breathed holding her up. "Oh thank you."

"Chris." She smiled, her eyes half shut. "We…"

"Shh." He quietened her; she was obviously weak and lacking energy. "It's ok. You can rest."

"Noo." She shook her head. "You… not…"

Charlotte wasn't making sense. Christian slipped her arm up round his shoulder, keeping her standing. "Chris." She tried again. Her brain was befuddled with such a sleepy numb state. She had to try to warn him. "You – not safe."

He helped to keep her steady as she swayed. "It's ok." He reassured her. "You knocked him out. You were a prize fighter. It will be fine."

Charlotte tried to focus her blurry vision. Chris's smiling face doubled and divided before her eyes. Oh why did she feel so sleepy? She wasn't exactly positive what was happening. A strange feeling had overpowered senses within her. A kind of numbness spreading throughout her limbs, her head felt so heavy. She had never felt so ill before, not even when she had a terrible flu. She could feel Chris's strength holding her up. "Thanks." She felt her head fall on to his shoulder as she mumbled.

"For what?" Christian's soft Irish lilt filled her ear. "It should be me thanking you."

"No." Charlotte put a lot of energy into speaking, draining her of the ability to do much else. How she managed to pull herself up earlier to take out Lettenby's evil soul was a mystery. All she could recall was hearing their voices. Chris and Lettenby breaking through her misty haze. It was enough an incentive to pull her to her feet. "Want to help."

"I know." Chris slipped his hand right around her waist and took more of her body weight. "You did brilliantly."

Dropping her gaze she could see Lettenby's bulk laying beneath them rasping. His snoring was horrendous; a warthog-like grunt followed each time with an incredible snort. And she thought her dad's nocturnal noise was bad. Never would she complain again.

Tim and Justin were lying on the ground; their bodies still with the overpowering drug. Charlotte felt for them, she really did. It was an underhand thing to do, drugging them all so they couldn't help their friend. It was only pure strength of will that had enabled Charlotte to do anything.

"Sarah." She remembered as Chris helped her walk over to the sleeping victims. "Got to… free…"

"Yes." Chris nodded. "We have to get you all home first. Escape whilst Lettenby is out cold. That was some whack you dished out but it won't keep him unconscious forever. It's better to have you all well and then we can really fight."

Reluctantly Charlotte could see the sense in what he was saying, well she was trying to but it was becoming increasingly difficult to stay awake. Chris sensing her weakened state bent to shake Tim and Justin into enough of a conscious state for them to make an escape. Whilst he could cope with Charlotte, he doubted he could cope with Justin and Tim all falling on him.

Having woken enough, the team blearily made their way through to the vortex before Lettenby woke. The four stumbled out of the vortex on the other side, slightly the less for wear. Tim, who had come round somewhat more than the rest of them, quickly took charge of the situation. "Charlotte." He held out his hands and took her from Chris who had been doing a good job of keeping her upright. "Oh please say you're all right."

Charlotte, who was more dazed than either Justin or Tim seemed to be, tried to speak. The throw which Lettenby had impacted on her had left her bruised. "Sarah…left."

"It's ok." He told her. "We'll get her next time."

Justin who was rubbing his eyes jumped when Tim shouted to him. "Help me get her downstairs." He had already opened the attic door. He ignored Christian who had actually been looking after her for the past half an hour.

Chris narrowed his eyes. "Want me to help?"

"No." Tim snapped, watching as Charlotte took her first wobbly step leaning on Justin, who wasn't exactly looking too bright himself, for support. "I think you've done enough."

"What?" Christian could hardly believe his friend's attitude. "What have I done?"

"Only put us all in danger." Tim glared over his shoulder. "Again. You should have warned us that Lettenby could hurt us like that."

"I didn't know." Chris wailed. "I had no idea."

"Well you should have done."

Turning his attention back to Charlotte, he helped Justin get her down the stairs.

The three of them were slightly shocked to see a figure standing in the main hall waiting for them. Well Tim and Justin were, Charlotte was still a bit too dazed to take in the severity of it. Shooting concerned glances over her head, the boys decided to play it by ear.

A dark shadow waited impatiently as they drew near. "Where on earth have you been?" Callum began furiously. "Mum sent me to get you, it was so late. I hope you know how mad…"

He broke off as he took in his sister's state. "Charlotte?" His eyes were huge. "What have you done to her? She looks wrecked."

"Uh we went on a bit of a walk. We're all pretty tired and Charlotte started to come over funny a while back." Justin half lied, trying to stand Charlotte up a bit more on her own to make it look slightly better.

"Yes the walk was a bit longer than we expected." Tim took up Justin's excuse. "We all got lost and then Charlotte started feeling sick…"

"Baloney." Callum burst into what he was saying. "You tell me what you've done to my sister now! And don't even bother telling me it was a walk that got her like this."

"It was." Justin sounded indignant. "Kind…"

"Oh shut up." Callum, seeing his sister's eyes half close, lunged forward and snatched her away from them. "You're not going to tell me the truth. Where's the nearest phone? I need to call our mum and dad."

"Don't." Charlotte moaned, the sound of her parents bringing her round slightly.

"Don't tell mum and dad!" Callum spluttered. "Are you totally nuts? You roll home hardly able to stand up and you don't think our parents are gonna get suspicious."

"Don't feel well." Charlotte doubled over attracting her brother's attention, stopping him mid-flow. "Please Callum."

"Yeah. Alright." Callum's face suddenly looked worried, he frowned. Helping her stand, he took in her pale face. "You really started to feel ill on a walk? They're telling the truth? You haven't been up to anything?"

"No." She groaned as she felt the room spin. "Got to sit down."

"No you don't." He slipped her arm over his broad shoulder and walked her to the door. "I'm taking you home. You can go to bed."

"If you're sick." He told her mimicking their mother. "Then you should be at home where you can get better."

Charlotte, normally always ready to fight him, quietly let him lead her out. "You ok?" He grunted as they descended the steps on to the front grounds. Her quietness was a sure sign that all was not well. His normal sister would have punching him in the arm and trying out her new kick boxing moves on him by now if he had even tried to get her to do something she didn't want to do.

"Mmm, just feel sleepy."

Callum shot her a quick look. "Yeah." Her pale face was not such a good sign either; her eyes were so unfocused that she looked very out of it. "Um Lotts, you would tell me if you'd done anything you shouldn't?"

"Yes." She nodded for once appreciating her brother's toned body to support her; his muscles giving her extra much needed help. "I'd tell you."

* * *

Tim and Justin, much to Mrs Bloom's surprise, went to their rooms that afternoon. After satisfying both their sisters' curiosity and answering that yes they had in fact found where Sarah was or, rather whom she was being kept hostage by, and that no they hadn't managed to free her. Both boys retired to bed for a long and much needed nap.

Christian sat in the attic and brooded. So many questions were floating round his head. How had Lettenby come back? It just hadn't been possible. The elder of the spectral world had made sure of that. There was simply no way.

Lying back in the dusty room, Christian remembered Lettenby's evil mocking face. How could anyone forget? Those eyes, one look at them and they burned their way into your brain forever.

All that cruel stuff that he had spouted, out of it all there was one thing that had stuck in his mind. He had questioned his trust in his friends. What had he meant? It seemed silly to even question it. Lettenby was trying to weaken him, split him from him his friends. It was with a guilty soul that he found himself re-examining his friendships, frantically trying to find the answer.

5

Guilt

Charlotte opened her eyes a little, just to help her see who had opened her bedroom door.

"Hey Sis." Callum was keeping his voice low, practically whispering. "So how are you feeling?"

"Fine." She sat up and instantly regretted it. The side of her body that had suffered the impact ached terribly. To top it all off she had developed a full-blown cold. "Urgh. Maybe I better lay back down."

"Um yeah." Her brother actually looked concerned. "Sleep. Mum said you should get plenty of rest."

Ever since he had brought her back the other day and the doctor had been called, he had been extra careful around her. She couldn't believe he was acting so sensitively. Maybe it was the idea that he had been so difficult with her before that was making him act with extra care now. He might have been feeling a smidgen of guilt but then again with Callum who knew?

"You're very lucky there's no school." Did she say he was acting sensitively? Well sensitively for her brother.

"Yes." She coughed. "Maybe I'll go out tomorrow. If mum'll let me."

"Yeah." He shuffled from one foot to another looking awkward. "Ok. Maybe I better go Do you want anything?"

"No." She sneezed. "Actually yes."

He halted at the door. "What?"

"Did Tim call today?"

"What?"

"Tim." She tried again reaching out for yet another tissue. "I thought I heard the phone earlier."

"Oh." Feigning innocence he shrugged.

Actually, she had heard much more than just the ringing. Waking her from her nap, wrenching her from her dreams of Elder Wood and the mysterious Lettenby, she had heard her brother on the phone and the sound of her name being mentioned and Tim's as well. Her brother deserved a chance to explain first.

"So?"

"No." He turned to leave.

"Callum."

"What?" He sounded frustrated.

Shooting him her best sister look murmuring. "You would say..." She started, interrupted by a few sneezes adding to her general sickly air. "If he had phoned?"

"Of course." He shrugged. "Yeah."

Charlotte moaned and reached up to her forehead. "Oooh I think I've got another temperature."

Stomping back over,Callum felt her forehead. "No." He started to say. "You'r.."

Before he could finish she looked up at him, all weak and defenceless. "Please Callum."

He rolled his eyes. "Oh ok." He sighed. "Fine Timothy did call. He wanted to see how you were."

"Why didn't you..?"

"I didn't want to bother you. You were asleep." He explained indignantly. "What? You expect me to come storming in here every time the phone rings?"

"Uh yes." She sighed. "When it is for me."

"Yeah.." Shifting from one foot to the other, he dropped his gaze to the floor indicating that she was not going to like what he said next. "Well I handled it."

"You handled it how?" Charlotte couldn't hide the questioning tone from her voice. Knowing her brother too well.

Callum avoided looking at his sister directly. A sign that he was definitely trying to hide something. Charlotte felt her suspicions rise.

She was about to ask what exactly he said to poor Timothy when her mother started to shout. "Callum!"

"Oops." He grinned, saved by his mother's not so calm tones. "Sorry. I gotta go."

"Don't you dare." Charlotte tried to sit up and reach out to stop him but he was too quick for her. With a smug smile he sped his way out of the room, high tailing it out the door.

Groaning Charlotte sunk back into her mattress. Sitting up quickly had not improved her giddiness. Instead she let her burning eyes fall closed and tried not to think of how awful her brother had been to her friend. Poor Timothy. He didn't deserve the anger of her brother. They had enough to deal with trying to win against that horrible Lettenby.

Deciding that enough was enough, she tried to get some rest and get herself back on form. The cold had to get better. She had no time to waste. After all, the boys couldn't deal with that evil head all on their own.

She wouldn't let them have all the fun. It wouldn't be at all fair.

Timothy sat in the kitchen staring glumly into his breakfast cereal. The flakes soaking up the milk and turning rapidly into soggy congealed flaps of golden mush. His eyes regarded the food soullessly as thoughts of the situation which he was in rushed through his heavy head; it was in such a mess. Everything had tumbled down around him. It had been like a domino effect. That one decision had been a catalyst to so many problems. If only he had not been so secretive. So ready to keep things quiet.

Lettenby. Oh he was the cause of so much misery. He should have guessed that the fiendish spirit would never rest until he had hurt them all. Hiding those cufflinks had been a big mistake.

A terrible misjudgement which had lead to so many disasters. If he had been honest with his friend... but no. He had to sit back watching Christian's sister going missing. Still he said nothing. Instead deciding to lie to his friend, not to trust his instincts and confide his troubles. If he had talked about his discovery sooner then maybe Christian could have done something about it. He wasn't sure what had stopped him. On so many occasions Christian and himself had put their heads together and overcome the relentless evil hearted monster.

It was just this time... this time he was so tired of the ongoing battle between good and evil that he just wanted to forget. To be 'normal'. Not to have constant worries about ghoulish ghosts coming back from the spirit world to haunt him. He knew that other kids his age never had such problems. The things they worried about were not getting into the football team or, horror of horrors, not having the right kind of trainers. Superficial worries like that were never top of Timothy's list because ever since he had moved to Elder Wood something had awoken inside him. A something which had lead him to some of the most wonderful adventures of his life but also a unique gift that had lead him into battles which had quite frankly opened his eyes to places he never believed existed.

People talked about special talents, he remembered his mum proudly pouring over a James Coats the night before, the maths genius who had enrolled into their school. On and on she had gone about what a special talent he had. She had told Mr Bloom what a smashing lad he was. The whole time Tim had sat there with Justin, a bitter feeling brewing inside him. There was a name for it. Jealousy. He had actually been jealous of this boy, someone he didn't really know and not because of his so-called special ability. No, what he was jealous of was the fact that he got to talk about his talent to everyone, anyone he liked. All the pupils knew about his talent and whether they liked it or not it was generally accepted. Something he knew he just couldn't be.

The previous night jealous thoughts had kept him feeling furious. Angry at the injustice of it all. Why should James be given all the glory and he be lumbered with a talent that earned him an awful lot of hard work and hardly any gratitude, well not on a grand scale anyway. It just did not seem fair. When God was handing out the extra talents did he get to Tim and decide that, oh no, Master Bloom could cope with all the added pressure of living a double life? That he should have this unique talent which will, by all intents and purposes, see him sorting out the problems of many spirits and ultimately oversee that good won over evil? Without any notoriety? Did he not think that the lives of eleven-year-olds was not pressured enough?

People like James could live an easy life with socially accepted gifts but Tim he was in the minority. Of course, feeling like this only made him feel more guilty. He knew that other people shared his talent, unique others. Charlotte for one, had the ability. Just thinking about her made his insides feel funny. After all she was so much better at handling these little problems. He had never met anyone so special before. She was so pretty but apart from that she knew how to handle herself. Ghosts never frightened her. Something which he wished he could boast himself. Whenever she was around him all he wanted to do was make her understand how much he liked her. Instead what he had done was land her in a heap of trouble.

He had been indulging in his problems. Meanwhile he had let his friends down. He had to learn that his special gift would be with him forever. He thought, and yes it had been mistakenly, if he kept the whole thing quiet, pretended that it did not exist then maybe it would all go away. Yeah right. Like problems went away like that in real life. No, what was that saying his mum always drummed in to him? 'Honesty was the best policy'. Well it certainly would have been if he had been able to tell the truth to his friend.

He had started off a spiral of events that he simply no longer had any control over. Squirming on his chair, he tried to ignore the weird feeling which had overtaken his tummy for the past few days. It was a niggling twinge, an incessant pain. He had only had it once before, a similar problem when he was five and had hastily devoured two cookies from the sacred biscuit tin. He had been told strictly to keep away from the coveted blue jar but like many five and a half-year-olds, temptation had got the better of him. The delicious choc chip stolen treat had been very good. However, a few minutes after the biscuit chunks had been sent down their way to his tummy, Tim felt the first twinges of dread. A something which his mum had gone on to see written all over his face. When Tim had questioned her lightly what had made it so obvious his mother had replied. "Guilt. Why Tim you told me what you had done yourself. I could see it as plain as day." Guilt. So that, he discovered, was what guilt felt like.

It was guilt which was stopping him eat. Keeping him awake. His lies had caused them all to have to go across to the other side to find Sarah. Put everyone in danger and made Charlotte so sick.

"Hey." A heavy pat on his back brought Tim out of his deep ponderings. "You're up."

"I couldn't sleep." Tim focused on Justin as he sat opposite him looking bright and happy.

"I know all about it." His friend grinned. "I heard your door opening in the middle of the night and then again at five in the morning."

"I went to get a glass of water." Tim explained. "Then I went back to bed, still couldn't sleep so went down to the kitchen for a snack but Mia Valtner must be moonlighting."

"Why?" Justin smiled relieved to see his friend making a fairly good attempt at humour.

"Well she must have a job at the secret service or something the way she hides the snacks. I searched every cupboard and I still couldn't find the crisps."

Justin grinned. "Yeah maybe they have a special branch for housekeepers at the good old MI5 building, training them up in the finer arts of food deception."

Tim managed to smile.

"That's better." Justin reached for the box of cereal and poured some into an empty bowl. "I thought you'd forgotten how to lift the corners of your mouth up, you've been looking so glum lately."

"Yes." He sighed. "Sorry."

"Don't worry about it." Pouring out some milk he tucked in heartily. "You've been... mphh mphh... trying to deal with a lot."

Watching his friend eat gave Tim slightly more of an appetite. Attempting to finish his own, he started to spoon up the remaining flakes that had turned to sludge.

"So have you spoken to Christian yet?" Justin asked. "Only he must have been upset about the other day."

"Yes." Tim shrugged non-commitedly.

"Is that a yes to the spoken to him question or a yes to agree that he is upset?" Justin couldn't pretend that he hadn't noticed how weird his friend had been acting whenever Christian was around. So protective of Charlotte.

"He's upset." Tim busied himself with an apple from the fruit bowl Mia Valtner had laid out extra early. She had even beaten him to the kitchen at six in the morning. That woman was something else. Always around when you least expected her and popping up in the most unlikely places. "I didn't want to add to his worries."

"Which roughly translates to you chickened out."

"No."

"It does."

No one knew him better than Justin. Tim relented slightly under his friend's steely gaze. "Ok. I chickened out."

"Why?" Justin finished his cereal and grabbed a slice of toast from the rack. Mia always laid out a feast at each meal time, enough to serve an army if they so happened to descend upon Elder Wood.

"I was rotten to him." Tim mumbled. "I practically ignored him."

"I was meaning to ask you about that." Justin crunched his way through a pear whilst buttering his toast. "Why have you been so mean to him lately?"

This was it. Honesty. If he wanted to talk about what he had done… "I"

"Tim!" Came the high pitched squeals that were only discernible to the ears of dogs and unfortunate older brothers. Mayhem spread its way through the kitchen as the little sisters came running through the door. "You're up. Goody."

Justin rolled his eyes in desperation.

"We need to talk." Louise told both boys firmly.

"Oh do we?"

"Yes." She curled her hair behind her ears in a business-like way. Both Kim and herself took seats. Sat down. Looked their brothers in the eyes. "We have to do something about Sarah."

"We had a think." Kim took over. "We as sisters, know how that poor little girl must be feeling."

Justin's eyes were huge and unbelieving. "Oh right."

"We do." Louise shot him a look.

"Oh yep." Tim agreed flashing Justin a serious glance. "They know all about being held hostage by spirits."

"I do actually." His sister complained, referring to

her own brush with Lettenby what seemed a lifetime ago. "I know exactly."

"Yes ok." He turned his attention to her thinking back to their previous experiences. "So you have first hand experience. What exactly do you suggest?"

"Well." Kim began. "We thought we could launch an attack."

"Launch an attack?" Justin was obviously fighting hard not to laugh. "What like in Saving Private Ryan. You do know that none of us have bullet-proof vests?"

"Don't be silly." She whacked him with the piece of toast he had buttered earlier. "I'm not talking mortal combat here, more territorial mind games."

"Where are you getting this stuff from?" Tim was astounded at the little girl's language.

Justin narrowed his eyes in disgust. "You haven't been reading my 24 series again have you?" He accused his little sister. The last time Kimberly had got her hands on the tense action packed novels, she had tried to imitate the hero Jack Bauer to the point of no return. It had landed her in a lot of trouble at school. In full stride he continued. "Because you know what mum said about going through my stuff."

"I haven't." She pulled a pained expression. "I do have better things to do with my time."

"Good." He didn't look like he believed a word of it.

"So." Tim brought the topic back to where it should be. "You both have an idea?"

"Yes a particularly good one." Louise agreed. Her eyes were sparkling with relish. "I think we should play on Lettenby's lust for revenge."

"How?"

"Simple."

"We make him think he's won."

"What?" Both boys were aghast.

"We let him do all the work." Kim, obviously aggrieved at her brother's lack of intelligence, spelled it out for him. "Let him lead us to Sarah."

"Then POW!" Lou slammed her fist down on to the kitchen table for emphasis and then regretted her decision. "We get him." She summed up, eyes watering and slightly ruining the powerful effect.

Tim hastily rose to his feet. "Ok." He summed up. "Let's get this plan into action."

Both girls jumped to their feet for once not even vying for the chance to fill their tummies. Giggling in glee with the excitement of having everyone act out a plan that they had created.

"What?" Justin stared at him. "You're actually going to go through with the girls' plan?"

Tim nodded.

"But you don't know what it entails. Even if it's plausible."

"We have to take action. We don't have much of the half term left." He shrugged. "Why not this?"

"Exactly." Louise took place beside her brother. "We've been letting Lettenby call the shots for far too long."

"Ok." Justin gave up the fight. "Let's do this."

6

The Good, the Bad and the Downright Dirty

The children hurried to group together in the Lost Sister Headquarters, which in reality was Timothy's bedroom but hey anywhere was better than nowhere at all. The girls sat on the bed whilst the boys stood by the window trying to work out all the meticulous details of the exact plan.

Timothy had been trying to send out a telepathic message to his friend but Christian was either way out of range or simply ignoring him. After their recent fights and bad patches Tim feared that it was probably the latter which was causing him to keep away. It was difficult to arrange all the angles of the plan without him but the children tried their best.

Knowing that the evil headmaster had control of the scenario was one thing but actually going in, beating him and retrieving Christian's sister was quite another. The general feeling between the children was one of anger and hot resentment but Timothy tried to keep a rein on the drastic measures the girls wanted to take their plan to. "I really think we need to impose some order." He tried in vain to shout over their enthusiastic suggestions.

"Kick him into next year." Louise rallied.

"No." Kim disagreed. "Let's capture and torture him for the rest of our lives."

"Will you two be quiet for a sec!" Both boys yelled at them.

"Please." Tim tried in a softer tone, noting the alarming stubborn features starting to form in his sister's face. Once set in her hissy fits, she could go on for a decade. "We just need to be a bit calmer about this. You're welcome to suggest ideas, so long as they do not include:

- Torture
- Physical fighting of the permanent injury variety
- Attack plans which involve bodily danger."

"Oh." Louise moaned. "You're no fun."

"This is stupid." Kim agreed. "We need some physical revenge."

Justin and Tim both stared open mouthed at their blood crazed younger siblings. Their fight-lust way out surpassed any that they had.

"No." Tim finally managed to splutter. "We do this seriously. Or not at all."

Louise stuck her tongue out. "Spoil sport!"

"Louise." Tim murmured. "Either you play by my rules.."

"Ok." She relented. "Fine but don't blame me if everything goes pear shaped. I'm not the one who's chicken about fighting."

"Noted." He turned back to Justin. "Never let those two near your computer games. They'll become monsters."

"I won't." Justin enthused, imagining what the two girls would be like after half an hour of gory graphics action. They were bad enough without any extra technological improvement.

With that matter aside they decided to take the first matter in hand. They needed something to lure Lettenby with.

Two evil eyes blinked in the moonlight. Total dark encompassed the surrounding misty land. Swirls of white started to rise up from the ground smoking their way up to the head of ink-like shadow. Black ice cold tendrils stretched precariously up, gathering strength as they moved. Ominous howls pierced the air and barks of anger burst out, small eruptions of feeling into the cold night air.

Struggling to free herself, Sarah moaned against the tight binds. It was no use. She was trapped. Looking around at the deserted woodland, she felt so alone. The acres of tall trees and gloomy light caused her heart to miss a beat. Who would find her? Out in the middle of a forest, she wasn't even sure where she was.

Wolfgang, who had been playing about in the mud, suddenly stopped as if he had been struck by lightening. He threw back his loveable huge head and howled...

It took everyone by surprise. The family pet, good old Wolfgang just didn't do that. Howling was not something he had done an awful lot of in his life.

Barking? Oh yes. Regularly.

But howling? Nope. Not normally. Only when there was a reason.

Everyone came to the same conclusion. There was something wrong. There just had to be.

The adults of course went about their daily business. To them a dog and his senses were prioritised fairly low on the list of irregularities.

The girls hurried to join the boys at the window eager to see what had caused all the mayhem downstairs. Tim frowned. "We better go down and see what is wrong with that dog of ours."

"Do you think he's come?" Louise asked with wide eyes, referring to Lettenby. Everyone knew that Wolfgang was one of the first members of the Elder Wood clan to notice their arch-enemy's presence. Many a time had seen the loyal hound picking up the first scents of the horrible soul before anyone had seen him.

"He might have." Tim did not want to rule any possibility out. He had learnt at Elder Wood that nothing could ever be taken at face value. "Let's go."

The children raced down the stairs in a mad dash. Tim was first to fall out on to the garden steps. It was a good job Mrs Bloom was not doing her rounds through the school or all four would have been told off for speeding through the building where all manner of hazards could befell them. Bumping into him quite hard came Justin, head first and so forcefully that he nearly sent poor Timothy into a nearby flower bed.

However, on seeing the garden, both boys' faces fell. The dog was nowhere to be seen. The girls, far from being put off the search, jumped down the last few steps and headed straight for the cluster of trees at the far side of the lawn... "He's probably headed off into the woods." Louise called out. "Come on!"

The four intrepid explorers began to push twigs

and branches out of their way. Faces were brushed with leaves and feet were pricked with sticks but still they pursued their canine buddy. The sound of distant howls drew close as Louise led the search. Hardly stopping to check if her companions were following, she frantically threw herself into the heavy bush and bracken eager to find their dog.

Tim tried to put his fears to the back of his mind. Ok so they were heading slightly further out into the wilderness than they were supposed to do. The more they ventured the darker it got. Tall trees formed Gothic archways over their heads; shadowy cloaks of black fell over them all. Tim wanted to run. Who knew woods became so spooky in the daylight? His only saving grace was that there was safety in numbers. Wasn't there? He hoped so.

They had had a torrential rain storm the night before. The rain had turned the formerly hard ground into mush. "There!"

The shriek had Tim jumping a foot in the air and grabbing for his friend's hand. Realising that it was too late he saw that it was his little sister who had screamed. Justin shot him a funny look as he released his hand. Embarrassment floored him. Get a grip, for Heaven's Sake.

"What's where?" He tried to sound gruff and brave.

"Dog." Louise spoke slowly and loudly. Her brother could be such an absolute riot. "Over there."

"Right." He shoved his way to the forefront of the line. "Great. Everyone stand back."

"Why?" Louise was fighting him for the right to stay in first place. "I can handle it Tim."

"No." He set his own expression, trying to look every inch the older brother. "I have to do this."

Looking sulky, Louise stepped aside. Tim eased the shrubs out of his way. All the overgrowth was probably the home to hundreds of rabbits and foxes. A somewhat comforting thought as he looked out into the barren field in front of him. The land was backing on to the small wood and belonged to one of the archaic Easy Ridge farmers and their families. Tim knew he was trespassing as he heaved himself up and over the rickety fence. He could see his dog sitting in the clearing just in front. It was his moment to make a decision. Was he going to do it? A quick look at the faces of Justin and the sisters told him. He had to.

"I can't see anything." He called back over his shoulder to them. "Just Wolfgang. Him and a bunch of black birds."

"Flock." Kim corrected.

"Yes." Louise continued primly. "A flock of birds."

"Ok." Tim groaned, wondering why he had to be saddled with two annoying girls. "Whatever. There isn't anything to get him so scared."

"What nothing?" Louise moaned. "Move out the way. Tim."

Barrelling through she knocked into him. Hard. "Ow!!"

"Don't be a baby." Louise turned scornful eyes on her older brother. "You don't feel anything? And I don't mean that tiny scratch. Nothing ghostly?"

"No." He replied coldly, feeling like he wouldn't tell her even if he did. Then he remembered that they were all supposed to be on the same side. He relented. "Nothing. I don't even feel anything remotely spiritual."

Louise studied the scene. Her eyes screwed shut. "No." She concluded. "I don't either."

Hey since when could she feel ghosts? Tim wanted to laugh but he stopped himself. Scorning her now would only mean trouble.

"There's nothing for you to do but to go over and get him." She decided. "Off you go."

Tim was reluctant to do so. Looking at the hound sat stubbornly in the mud, he had visions of them rolling around in the earth before he could get him anywhere near the house. That dog did funny things when he got a spiritual whiff or scent. Suddenly he had an idea. "Wolfgang!" He shouted.

Nothing. The dog remained rigid. Not even a wagging tale to be seen.

"Come on." Tim called hanging over the fence precariously. An inch further and he would topple over. Head first into the mud. Knowing him.

"Wolfi." He pleaded. "Come home."

"Tim." Louise moaned. "Will you get on with this. You have to go get him. He'll never come back on his own, you know what he's like when he's sensed something other worldly."

Jumping down Tim sighed. Here we go. "Good dog." He spoke quietly. "Have those ghosts been popping up again? Winding you up."

Wolfgang whined.

With his audience firmly stood behind the fence, Tim went on gently. The girls and Justin strained to see exactly what was going on. No doubt they would find him being thrown in the mud a hilarious situation. Tim wasn't going to let that happen. Not a chance.

"Come here." He stepped easily round his large good natured friend. "Wolfgang?"

The dog was gazing out at the middle distance. Waving his hand in front of the dog's eyes still did not catch his attention at all. Weird. Tim reached out his hand to him. Things seemed to be easy so far, nothing too surprising. Wolfgang could act strangely at times and Tim supposed living in a haunted house was stressful for any animal. These little flake-outs were to be expected. As his fingers reached his dog's fur he was about to take hold of the situation when he felt that he was being talked about. He looked up and almost instantly his suspicions were confirmed.

His audience remained quiet apart from Louise who, with her face turned towards his friend, was whispering frantically. No doubt about how her methods were far more successful at tackling their dog. Rolling his eyes at Justin they both grinned and that's when Wolfgang decided to jump.

7

Mystery Clue

The world span. Literally. Poor Tim was pulled across the grass on his bottom straight into the mud by an excited Wolfgang. Splatters of icky brown sludge showered from left and right as the little boy was towed directly through an overgrown bush. With a thud he was deposited with reckless abandonment. Quickly avoiding the dog's trampling feet, he sat up and rubbed his head.

"You ok?" Justin shouted to him.

"Of course he's ok." He could hear Louise laughing. "His clothes aren't though. Mum is going to be furious."

Getting to his feet Tim was not in a good mood. "Wolfgang." He ordered the panting dog. His tone said he meant business but the hound hardly flinched, he was so confident.

Brushing the mud off his trousers, he groaned. His original feeling had been right. Following the dog in his current state had only headed him into trouble. Scowling at his mirth-filled little sister he reached out to grab Wolfi's collar and was tugged rather roughly across the field and into the woods.

"Tim!" His friends and sister called.

He could do nothing to stop the trip though. He was helpless. It was like being strapped into a heart stopping, fast, adrenalin-filled ride at a theme park. Tim was gripping on for his life.

Rushing past greenery at a hurtling speed did nothing to settle his stomach. Finally managing to let go, he fell coughing into a deep dark patch of grass overshadowed by trees. "Ooh." He moaned as he gazed forlornly at his red raw hands. Another injury to add to his collection.

Blinking in the half-light he looked around for his dog. There was nothing. Nothing apart from trees. Oh and that girl. She did look slightly odd.

What? Turning back he studied the ghostly apparition.

"Sarah?" He rose shakily to his feet.

Charlotte sneezed and wiped her nose. "Please." She tried again. Appealing to her brother's good side. "Just for a half an hour."

"I told you." He turned his back on her. "No."

"Callum." She tried to reason. "It will not be out of your way."

"I don't care." He told her slowly adjusting his helmet. "I'm not taking you to see him."

"You wouldn't be?" She groaned. "I can take myself. Mum would be more comfortable if you accompanied me on the bike ride to Elder Wood. You know what she's like about me riding alone."

"Tough."

"Hey." She moaned, sneezing again. "This isn't fair."

"Life's not fair." He swung himself on to his bike. "Now go back inside and rest."

"I will not."

"Fine." He started to cycle down the hill. "Then get worse. Let your cold get so bad that you can hardly get out of bed again."

Stomping her foot on the ground Charlotte felt childish. "See", she felt like shouting, "This is what my older brother does to me". Who said being an only child was no fun? Right now a life without Callum seemed terribly appealing.

Watching him cycle expertly down the steep incline and flip his front wheels into the air whilst he teetered back she felt the firm grip of strength coil in her stomach. The same one which would always lead her into battle. Oh well. Checking back at the house she peeped through the bottom of the kitchen window and could see that her mum was busy doing the dishes.

What problems would it really cause if she cycled off without big brother to keep an eye on her? She had the bike. It was staring her in the face. A gleaming red BMX which she had been given last Christmas. It would take her under half an hour to cycle to Elder Wood. She could be back by dinner. After all, she wasn't a baby. She could handle a cycle on her own.

Timothy gasped as he saw what a predicament Sarah was in. Drawing closer he saw just how badly she had been tied up. How on earth could Lettenby do this? "It's ok." He reassured her. "I'll go get help."

Sarah closed her eyes. Her arms were tied up in the most intricate knots Tim had ever seen. Her mouth gagged. Not to mention the eerie red fiery glow which encased her whole body. This was not going to be an easy one to figure out.

"Wait here." He said before thinking, then grinned. She couldn't go anywhere. "Sorry. I'll be back in a minute."

"You're here!" The girls cried when they saw him.

"All right mate" Justin slapped Tim on the shoulder and then looked at his own muddy hand in disgust. "Ew maybe we should get you back for a shower."

"No time. We've got to go back." Tim breathed.

"What? Lou moaned. "Through that mud?"

"Why?" Kim asked.

"I've found her." He knew his eyes must be huge. Three blank expressions stared back.

"Sarah."

"Oh."

"What?"

"Where?"

"Follow me." He turned tail and lead them back towards the spot.

The children worked their way as quickly as possible over the fence through to the woods.

Kim and Louise grumbling all the way. "My skirt is totally ruined."

"Stop moaning." Tim hissed at her. "We have to get to Sarah."

"We know." The girls chimed. "You don't have to tell us."

Wolfgang was standing guard over Sarah and barked as the four kids approached.

Obviously pleased for back up.

Tim ran over and checked on Sarah.

"Are you ok?"

"Mm."

"Sorry." He looked at the gag. "We'll try to get that off in a minute."

Sarah nodded.

"Come on." Kim jumped up and tried to get the material off her herself. "Let's get it off now. It looks uncomfortable."

"Don't be stupid." Justin piped up suddenly aware of his little sister's act of bravery. "No! Kim."

It was too late.

Kim had reached up on her tip-toes to reach the gag, her little fingers wiggling towards the taut piece of material. The tips of her fingers started to touch the ethereal light, recoiling slightly. It was far too late. The three children could only stare in horror as Kim's tiny fingers hit the red flames. They sizzled against the red orange glow. Moaning, her little body shook with the force before being flung violently through the air.

Silence ensued.

Sarah's eyes were big and round as she watched, almost instantly struggling with her binds.

Louise looked petrified.

Justin and Tim, snapping out of their daze, ran over to where Kim was laying in the grass having avoided hitting a tree.

"Oh my gosh." Justin sunk down on to his knees next to her lifeless body. "Kim?"

He reached out to touch her pale face but Tim grabbed his hand at the last minute. "No. Not until we know what happened."

"What?" Looking up at his friend Justin seemed bewildered. "I can't just leave her. She's my sister."

"I know." Tim felt his own gaze droop to where Kim was sleeping peacefully on the floor. Well she seemed to be sleeping but Tim knew it was probably far more serious. Electric shocks were, weren't they? That bolt of energy sure did look high voltage. "I just... we don't know what's happened."

"My sister's been electrocuted. He was shouting. "That's what's happened."

Tim tried to calm him down.

"You're scaring the girls."

Louise and Sarah looked about ready to pass out. Tim's sister was darting startled glances from Kim on the ground and then to Justin shouting at her brother.

Sarah was simply watching everything unfold with terror. Oh this was awful. She was in big trouble.

Lettenby had not let her go. Oh no, he had used her as a pawn in his game. Struggling, she felt the burning sensation of rope against her skin. Tim and that other boy were fighting.

A little way away she could see that poor girl. The one who had tried to help her. She was lying in the grass.

Where was her brother?

Christian.

Closing her eyes, she called for him hoping that maybe this time he would be able to come.

Charlotte cycled across the nearby pathway; she had been puffing for breath a while back. The busy neighbourhood streets were now long behind her as she swapped friendly tarmac for rough gravel footpaths.

Callum would have been half-way to the park by now; he was a mad keen bike rider. His destination, a recreational ground at the other side of the village. It was a deserted piece of green that the young generation had claimed as their own. Over the half term her brother had met a few of his mates down there quite a few times. Spending their time laughing, kicking a football around and generally feeling grown up.

Whizzing past a blur of green to her left, Charlotte prepared herself for the next leg of her journey. The toughest part. The hill. It was a notoriously busy stretch of road, well used by all the shoppers and inhabitants of Easy Ridge as it cut right through the heart of the village. Charlotte was ready for it though. Tackling tough situations was what she loved most.

Turning sharply to the right, the bike veered heavily towards the main road. With the sun beating down on her head, Charlotte felt very hot. Beads of sweat started to form on her forehead, she could only imagine what her hair was going to look like when she unclasped her helmet. Oh, 'helmet hair' was so not in.

Her mind drifted off at a tangent just like her bike as she hit the black felt main road. Horns blared making her jump. Behind her someone shouted, her head swivelled to hear but at the same moment a loud crash distracted her. A lorry unloading it's contents into a village shop started bleeping. Charlotte felt the panic start to rise in her. All the road safety talks her parents gave her started to filter through her brain. Look both ways. No wasn't that for pedestrians? Supposing it was for cyclists too, she did as she had been told. A hundred times before. The road was so busy. She hadn't anticipated so much traffic. The school holidays had certainly taken their toll; lines of cars sped past in both directions. Charlotte's head was constantly swivelling left and right like a spectator at a tennis match. Was it safe to venture out now? No maybe not. Huge Space Cruisers hurtled past catching Charlotte's breath. The intimidating size and speed of the traffic was enough to make her wish that she had her older brother with her. He was always telling her what to do, but when the roads were busy he was first to take the lead. Her parents, on this occasion were right.

Children on their school holidays were popping in and out of the shops on the far side of the road. Charlotte was actually able to spot a couple from Elder Wood. Familiar faces as they bought sweets and laughed with their friends. Seeing them reminded her of how much she wanted to be with her own friends. Tim would no doubt have been much further along with their plan to find Sarah. Waiting for the traffic to lighten was a total pain. Scanning the busy streets. Charlotte tried to keep cool and that's when she saw it.

Angelica Dreyford, their school headmistress was walking primly across the road. What was she doing here? Charlotte had always secretly had her suspicions about that woman, ever since she had overheard a conversation between her parents about their headmistress and some mysterious past. Everyone had secrets, she knew that. It was just Mrs Dreyford seemed to have more than most.

A while ago her husband had moved down to the village but he hardly ever seemed to be around. Always abroad on business, Charlotte was convinced that they never got to see each other. No, Mrs Dreyford was committed to her job. Married to it. Charlotte watched as she slinked her way past the shops without a glance to either side. She was definitely up to something.

The traffic lights turned amber and Charlotte

waited as they followed their sequence. The minute she saw red she regarded both lanes of traffic and then launched herself into the fray. Riding carefully, she waved at a few girls she knew from school keeping her eyes focused on the woman in front of her. It wouldn't hurt to see what she was up to.

Kim lay motionless on the grass, her pale face unflinching. The boys were arguing over her, raising their voices. Their rage echoing on the wind. "You shouldn't have let them come here."Justin was accusing Tim of being irresponsible. "Look at my sister. I've got to get help."

"No. Tim's arm shot out at the last minute grabbing his friend. "You can't. Give me a minute to work things out."

"What things?" Justin shook his head in disgust. "This is not something you can work out. The situation has gone too far."

"No." Tim was reluctant to relinquish his role of managing the situation. "Lettenby did this. If we could only..."

"Only what?" Justin took a step away from him. The birds had stopped chirping, the woods were silent except for the two boy's loud voices. "Call Lettenby here. Let him hurt us all some more."

"I won't let him."

Both boys swung round at the haunting Irish lilt.

"Christian." Tim sounded relieved. Justin surprised.

Sarah sounded her muffled joy.

Christian's eyes widened as he took her in. The relief washed over his face to be reunited with his sister.

Justin, who was still concerned about his own sibling groaned. "I don't want to cut this short but I need to do something about Kim. Now."

"Is she hurt badly?" Christian was over the middle ground in under a second. Leaning over Kim's body and studying it closely. "What happened to her?"

"It was that light." Louise suddenly ran forward coming out of her terror-induced daze. "That fire."

Christian looked at her. Then he regarded the glow surrounding his sister.

"Kim will be fine. It is not an electric shock." He reassured Justin. Then he turned to Tim. "We need to get her back inside."

Nodding, both boys started to lift Kim to her feet. "Wh..?" Opening her eyes she started to groan. Much to Justin's relief. "What happened?"

"Don't worry." Justin reassured her. "Everything's ok. You just had a little accident."

"Come on." Tim helped Justin take her back over to the fence. "We will get her back home and then meet up back here."

"That's fine." Christian nodded. "I'll stay here."

Louise joined her brother and the four traipsed to the manor.

Left alone, Christian ran over to his sister. "Oh." He sighed. "Sarah I'm so glad we found you."

His sister wriggled.

"Ma and Pa will be overjoyed." He reassured her. "Everything will be fine."

It was difficult standing next to his sister and yet not being able to help her in any way. The red glow grew stronger and more powerful the closer he got. Throbbing away with a frightening passion.

Christian knew that Lettenby had surrounded her with a small sample of his fury. Putting her here in the woods, leading Wolfgang to her. That had all been a trap.

The trouble is that, trap or not, Chris knew he had to free his sister. He couldn't leave her tied up and surrounded with Lettenby's hate. This was going to be the battle to end all battles. Christian could feel Lettenby's dark presence pulsating through the atmosphere. He was close. Extremely close.

Christian was ready, he thought he was.

8

Ghostly Power

Charlotte upped her pace. Frantically pedalling for all she was worth, the thought had crossed her mind that she could be an Olympic cyclist. She was definitely fast enough. On the other hand she could always choose a job in the private eye sector. Keeping a safe distance, she had been able to tail her headmistress all the way to the other side of the village. Without being noticed.

Angelica Dreyford was power-walking her way into the local cemetery. Odd destination. Especially for someone who had no roots in the village.

"We need to find Lettenby." Christian told them all. "He's the only one who can let Sarah out of this."

Justin, who had only just returned with Tim, looked sceptical. "Oh yes." He agreed. "We should just call upon this dark spirit and battle him ourselves."

"We've done it before." Tim argued.

"Look where that's got you." He held his friend's

gaze. "Lettenby's here isn't he. You couldn't get rid of him."

"We will this time." Christian's voice was strong. This was a saga that would come to an end. "Lettenby will not be bothering any of us again."

Boom!

The sound reverberated around the heads of all four children. Louise for once had chosen to stay with Kim back at the school ready to explain her need for a lie down to her mother. Sarah, Christian, Tim and Justin stood still. They knew what eerie source had caused it.

"Lettenby!" Christian walked into the clearing. "You show yourself now."

Sarah struggled against her binds. Tim and Justin exchanged looks. Whilst they wanted to get this over with, they were not so sure they wanted to come face to face with the evil lord yet again.

"I mean it." Chris was ranting. "I have had enough. You are not to sink your claws into anyone else. Not my friends, not my family. If you want me, come and fight."

There was a moment whilst silence ensued. Nothing moved; even the birds kept quiet and hidden out of the way. The boys stood firm. Slowly black clouds started to form, covering the sky at an alarming pace. A cold wind whipped up around the children. Darkness started to overshadow the light. Freezing drops of rain plopped from the sky which the children hardly felt; they were too busy focusing on the tiny black shadows which were swirling around in front of them. Gradually taking the shape of someone all four never wanted to see again.

The storm came out of nowhere. Huddling her coat around her, Charlotte blinked the rain out of her eyes. Huge drops were falling off her lashes onto her cheeks. Staring straight ahead she tried to keep Angelica Dreyford in clear sight. The woman had been gathering bits of twig and foliage from around a tomb-like stone. It was by far the most grand in the lot. Without getting too close and being noticed, Charlotte edged closer towing her bike behind.

Mrs Dreyford was kneeling in front of the huge marble stone in a prayer- like gesture. Holding her breath Charlotte trod lightly ever closer until she too could see the writing on the stone.

Dedicated to all the children and adults who lost their lives in the Elder Wood fire. She read. Lord A. Lettenby.

This didn't make sense. Of course the village would pay respect to such a tragedy but why was their head teacher so grief stricken at the prospect. Watching as she bent closer, she heard her headmistress whisper… "Don't worry Alexander, I won't let anyone ruin your plans."

Charlotte gasped.

Angelica whipped around and with eyes like lasers homed in on Charlotte. "What are you doing here?" She rapped out rising to her feet. "Were you following me?"

"No." Charlotte backed away. There goes the job as a private detective. "I was uh just… out for a ride."

"In the local cemetery?" Her headmistress smiled icily. Ew, there was the family resemblance. Charlotte felt her blood run cold, a feeling she had often read about in books and now truly understood. Surely this was a mistake? Angelica Dreyford was related in some way to Lord Lettenby? "I think not." The intimidating voice rose as she drew ever closer. "What are you doing here Charlotte? Explain now."

"I…" She started to say, watching the heavy rain plaster the older woman's hair to her head. Actually with the running mascara and the flat hair she was quite a frightening sight. "Really. I was just out for a ride. I wanted to go see Timothy."

"Now that I can believe." Mrs Dreyford stopped inches from her face. "You two have become quite inseparable. I often wonder why Mrs Bloom doesn't put a stop to it, I mean it can't be good for your studies can it? All these little distractions."

Charlotte shook her head, her eyes still locked on Angelica's shockingly oval shaped ones.

"I mean I wouldn't want to have to fail you on your work. Call those lovely parents of yours in." She smiled nastily. "Maybe you should keep that pretty little nose of yours out from where it is not wanted. Go home and keep away from Elder Wood apart from during school hours of course. I've been hearing bad reports about you and I wouldn't want to have to impose a suspension."

With a sense of surprise Charlotte tried to keep her mouth closed. She was a straight A student, never in trouble. Who had been dropping her in it?

"I mean it." Angelica had her up against a tree, water dripping on to them from overhanging branches. "Stay away."

"Charlotte?"

Never had she been so relieved to hear a familiar voice. Turning sharply, Mrs Dreyford regarded one of her other pupils and backed away.

"Hey Mrs D." Callum jumped off his bike and ambled over. "You should get out of this rain. It's getting worse and there are black clouds all over the park."

"Yes." She looked between the pair. "I will. Thank you."

"No probs." He regarded his sister. "What are you doing here?"

"Out for a ride." Angelica supplied icy eyes still on Charlotte's face. The warning was there. Loudly keeping her in her place. "I'm surprised your parents let her out so soon Callum. I heard she wasn't well. Timothy was extremely worried."

"She isn't." He took his sister's hand firmly. "I'll take her back home now. Get her back in the warm."

"Good idea. She will stay out of trouble there."

Callum pulled Charlotte and her bike over to the main road already swinging himself back on. "See you around Mrs D." He shouted unaware of the secret message she was transmitting to his sister.

Only Charlotte knew that there was a warning behind Mrs Dreyford's casual tone of voice. A lethal warning.

Christian closed his eyes against the strength of the wind which was whipping them all directly in the face. Icy fingers cut into their skin. "Lettenby!" Christian roared.

The black shadow which had caused so many nightmares appeared before them. Lettenby's cruel eyes regarded them all with a malicious smile. "How dare you." He spoke to Christian. "Order me out of my own school eh?"

"Let my sister go." Christian held the gaze with formidable strength. "This is not a fight to do with her."

"Oh my dear boy but it is." He turned his face to Sarah. "I will keep on until I rid all of your family.

111

So much like you. Surprising to see such idiotic foolishness run in a family. She was so easy to capture."

"You…" He launched himself at the spirit but Tim and Justin held him back.

"Not yet." Tim whispered in his ear.

"Remember what the girls said." Justin added. "Let him think he's won and then we can trap him."

"What are you three muttering about?" Lettenby swore. "You better not be planning anything? Not if you want Sarah to stay somewhere you can see her."

"Haven't you done enough?" Tim demanded. "Why can't you just move on."

"I do not want to." He regarded the boy coldly. "You think that your family moving in makes Elder Wood yours but it does not."

He stepped closer. "This is my school. It will always be mine. You and your friends can do whatever you want but I will not relinquish my right."

"Ok." Tim shrugged. "We may as well admit defeat."

"What?"

"Well." He caught the evil headmaster's eye. "If you're really as powerful as all that and you won't give up…"

"I will never give up."

"Fine." He smiled. "Then we will let you carry out your plan."

"You will?" The sharp black eyes narrowed in mistrust. "All of you?"

"Yep." He looked at Justin for confirmation. "All of us."

Lettenby looked puzzled. He could not believe that the children were going to let him win.

"Well." He lent on his carved cane. "I must say I did not think I would see the moment when Timothy Bloom and Christian Cortex gave up their fight."

Christian was struggling to keep his tongue firmly between his teeth. How he was going to stay quiet he just did not know.

"All right." Callum sighed when she had poured herself some hot milk. "What were you up to?"

"Me?" She took a sip calmly, her insides quivering. "Nothing."

"Oh so you just hang about the cemetery in the pouring rain for fun?"

"Yes." She turned her back on him hoping for some peace.

"Not to mention the fact that you went out on your bike on your own."

"So?"

"So you know how much trouble you would be in if mum and dad found out?"

"If they find out." Turning back to him she shot him an imploring expression. "You don't have to tell them."

"Don't even go there Lottie." He walked out of the kitchen. "I've been covering for you so much lately that I haven't had a chance to get up to anything myself."

"Oh perleease." She carried her milk behind him. "You know how over protective they are and I was fine."

"Yeah." He scoffed. "Fine standing out in the pouring rain in the middle of a cemetery."

"I was."

"Besides you might not have been all right out on

the road. I bet you rode on the High Street in the middle of all that traffic."

Charlotte looked away guiltily.

"I thought so." He laughed. "Anyway you wanted to go to school didn't you, to see lover boy. What happened?"

"Something came up."

"Something in a graveyard?"

"Yes."

"Sometimes I wonder about you." Callum shook his head. "I'm going to my room."

Mrs Bloom came out of her study and surveyed the large hall. Why on earth was it such a freezing temperature? Old buildings were difficult to keep warm but this was ridiculous. Pulling a second cardigan over herself she rubbed her arms. "I must call the plumber." She decided. "Maybe the central heating's packed up."

Rushing off, she walked straight into and through the other side of a very indignant Lord Lettenby.

The children met up in the library knowing full well that everything was up to play for. If they gambled and lost.. then life as they knew it would cease to exist. Lord Lettenby would be able to cause all sorts of mayhem.

Charlotte sat in her bedroom and, after changing her clothes into something far warmer and drier, thought about what she had seen. Their headmistress had something to hide but she had never guessed that it was directly linked to Lord Lettenby. It was atrocious. The very thought that someone from the

114

same family should rule Elder Wood. Once again.

Lifting the phone, she decided she had to tell Timothy and Christian at once.

The phone rang at Elder Wood, echoing through the large hall just as the front door swung open. A dripping wet hand reached for the receiver...

Kim woke from her nap. Louise had been staring out of the window wondering if their plan would work. The scare that Lettenby had given her earlier was enough to give her doubts about the strength of their plan.

Wolfgang and Suki were wandering idly through the hall when a shadow stopped them. Whining Wolfgang gazed on in shock. That evil spirit was standing in front of them.

"Suki!" Mrs Dreyford scolded the instant she howled. "Will you behave you fat creature."

The dog blinked up at her owner in bewilderment. Could she see the scary looking figure or was it just Wolfgang and herself who were witness to him? If so. they really should alert the children.

"Honestly." Angelica stepped forward and took her place beside Lettenby. "You must not act like that in front of family."

Family?

Wolfgang, tongue lolling out of his mouth, started to back away. This was not good. So not good.

Upstairs Miss Kitty Fiddle, the language teacher's parrot, ruffled her feathers. "Emergency." She called knowing something was about to happen.

Timothy and the boys carefully regarded each other. They had their plan firmly set. It would take the strongest acts of courage, trust and true friendship that they had ever shown in their lifetime. If they wanted to beat Lettenby then they would all have to work in unison. It was strangely appropriate that Tim should be facing Lettenby with both his best friends backing him up.

9

Test

Charlotte put the receiver down and jumped off the bed. Oh boy, they were in trouble. Racing to the door she bumped straight into her brother.

"Hey." He looked down at her and frowned. "What's up?"

"I've got to get to Elder Wood."

He groaned with emphasis. "Not again."

"Yes again." She tried to shove past him. "Will you ride with me?"

"No." He watched her struggling to shift him.

"Thanks." She rolled her eyes. "I have such a helpful brother."

"I can't." He told her. "I'm going to a party."

"Where?" Her eyes grew huge. Most of her brother's friends lived in the centre of the village, quite close to the hill that would take her to Elder Wood.

"Bridge Lodge."

"Great." She ducked under his arm and ran to the coat stand. "You can let me join you for the ride, it's on the way. Oh and I want to keep it quiet, I think mum's getting a bit suss about me spending so much time up there."

Her brother grumbled. "No kidding. You're spending more time at school during the holidays than we have to in a school term."

"I know." She smiled sweetly. "It will be worth it though."

Wolfgang licked at Suki's ear in a gesture of comfort. The poor female was cowering, tail firmly between her legs. This was a turn up for the books. Lettenby actually had family. A great, great granddaughter to carry on the family traditions. Angelica Dreyford. Who was better than a naturally cruel born heir? Stone hearts run in that family.

As if they didn't have enough to deal with, they now had yet another cold hearted nemesis to put in her place. Discouraged, the dogs tried to look brave. Wolfgang bared his teeth slightly at the ghostly headmaster, his lip curling in disgust. Even if they could not act the part at least they could look it.

Suki tried to support him with a throaty bark of her own. A sound which rewarded her with a sharp cane in the ribs. Breathing in, she let out a painful whimper. Her full belly constricted with a spasm; a burning flash of pain. A strange wriggling started to the right and moved all the way across her bump. Wolfgang, quick as a flash leapt forward in defence of his loved one and received a crowning kick to the head from Angelica.

"Keep quiet." The tone of voice was nothing if not frightening.

However the whole situation seemed to have

impressed Lettenby who looked upon his family member with proud eyes. "I am impressed Angelica. These days I rarely have the occasion to see such fine displays of physical control."

"Such a shame they've brought in new laws." She agreed. "I hear the corporal punishment of your day was excellent. I can think of a few children who could do with a harsh whipping to put them in their place."

"Only a few?" Lettenby took a seat at her desk. "My dear, in my highly distinguished view, all children can do with a few hard whacks to knock some sense into them. The things I've seen over the years. Parents pampering the young. Namby pamby ideals which result in chaos I tell you. Utter turmoil."

"Oh I quite agree." Shooting the dogs a long hard stare, she sat opposite her idol. "I am so glad you persuaded me to come here Grandfather Alexander. Together I have the feeling that we can really shape the education system into something worthwhile. No one else understands my views."

A few miles away Callum emerged from his bedroom in full costume. Well his idea of party gear.

"Oh my gosh!" Charlotte who had been waiting at the front door burst out giggling. "Could you not find anymore black to put on? Maybe a balaclava?"

"Ha ha." He strode over to her in his black bike boots. "Remember I am doing you a favour."

"Uh huh."

"I never asked for your opinion on my dress sense."

"Well you should." Charlotte regarded her brother's strange yet intriguing studded neck collar. "I never knew we had a dog."

Callum shot her a look of warning. "Lottie it's still not too late for me to call this off."

With resignation she called the teasing off. She was having so much fun that it was hard to stop but if she didn't she might jeopardise her escort to Elder Wood. "Ok."

"Mum, I'm off." Callum shouted out. "I'll be back at ten."

"Ok Love." Their mother's tone filtered through. "Have you seen Lottie? I haven't heard her since she went out earlier."

"Yes." He shot her a look. "I'm taking her with me."

"What to your friend's party?" She came through to the hall. "Won't that seem a little odd?"

"Nope." He lied. Normal circumstance would never see him letting his little sis tag along. "It's fine."

"Well ok." Their mother looked a little shocked. "Have a nice time."

"Bye." They both called as they hurried out.

Elder Wood was clouded in a veil of darkness. Huge black skies hung over the ancient building. A sense of doom evaporated through the exterior walls and out into the very atmosphere around the village.

Callum pulled up sharply on the shingles. He sent up a shower of gravel in his wake, Callum had insisted that he accompany Charlotte right to the door and as such walked up the steps with her.

"Whoa this place gives me the creeps." He put on this fake Count Dracula voice. "Rather you than me hoo hoo ha."

Charlotte rolled her eyes. Ironically her brother's

clothes were making him look a much more terrifying vision than Elder Wood. At the present time anyway.

"Well you can go."

"Yeah?"

"Yes."

"Right." He jumped back down the steps. "Meet me at the gates at nine-thirty."

She nodded.

"Nine-thirty." He repeated as he got on his bike. "I don't want to have to come in there and get you again. I spend enough time here without giving my school holidays up."

Charlotte sighed whilst her big brother launched himself back on to the main hill. His gothic attire was certainly going to win him points with his friends. Turning back to the situation, she gazed at the large door and gripped the handle.

Mrs Bloom cuddled baby Meg to her chest. "How are we feeling today Angel?"

The upstairs floor was strangely cool and uninviting. In fact the whole manor had become unwelcome. Brushing the feeling off she turned her attention to her baby. Her sister Pandora was much more of a believer in feelings of such a nature.

It was a comfort to know that all the other occupants of the house were busy. Safely consumed with whatever task they deemed fit to fill their holiday with. Chloe hated to have to organise everyone. Ok maybe she didn't hate it. She just thought that one should take an occasional break from the hobby of a long lifetime.

The other children seemed to have occupied themselves. Meg happily mumbled words she knew. String together a couple of numbers and she felt like the most intellectual person on the planet. Haphazardly telling her mother all about Lord Lettenby and the cufflinks she had found. "Ooh." She exclaimed. "Man. Naughty."

"Was he?" Chloe smiled at her infant's attempt at chatter. In a few months she would be much more advanced than she hoped. "That's nice dear."

"Noo." Her toddler could tell by her mother's expression that she had not understood the point she had gone to such lengths to describe. Deciding to go in for the 'actions speak louder than words' concept she slapped her mother on the head. "Man. Bad."

"No bad baby." Her mother corrected setting her back down in her cot. "Honestly what is Louise teaching you? She should have told you hitting is not acceptable."

The baby slapped her cot bars to be heard. Mrs Bloom, thinking she was overtired, tried to settle her down. "Meg is tired." She explained. "Needs to go bye-byes."

"No bye-byes." Meg shook her head as she saw a familiar shape over her mother's shoulder. "Loo!" She pointed. "Ba Man."

"No." Chloe Bloom looked behind her. "There is no one."

"No." The baby was furious. "Man!"

"No there is no man." She explained patiently. "Now go to sleep."

Lettenby bared his teeth at the baby, eager to scare her. Baby Meg, made of stern stuff, simply poked her tongue out at him blowing a raspberry.

"Megan." Her mother scolded.

"Brat." Lettenby followed.

The baby wasn't put off. She was still on her guard.

"Go!" She pointed a chubby wrinkled finger at the door.

"I will not go." Her mother was shocked. "That is no way to talk."

"Use your power. Punish her." Lettenby whispered in Chloe's ear. "Show her whose boss. Regain some respect."

Mrs Bloom flinched as the cold air shot against her skin. "I must get that plumber to come round." She thought out loud and then fitted a blanket around her daughter's tiny body. "Make the school feel a little less chilly when school starts."

Meg pretended to shut her eyes having realised that her mother was not able to see the same cruel eyes as she was able to. Instead she simply kept one eye half-open and focused on Lettenby.

The head started to come nearer. Baby Meg prepared herself. With a sharp finger she poked him in the eye, showing a good deal of Bloom spirit.

Angelica was simply delirious that the children had given up their fight so easily. "Stamina is what they lack." Her great, great grandfather had confided in her. "No staying power."

It meant that they could move on to the second stage of their plan. Following orders, she found Mrs Bloom in the nursery. Gently opening the door she waved to the woman and motioned for her to come out.

"Oh Angelica." Chloe slipped out of the room. "Good timing. Little Meg's just nodded off."

"How lovely." The headmistress tried to show willing. "They're simply adorable at that age; all cute smiles and dimples."

"Mm." Mrs Bloom, always eager to show her children off, started to tell her about the progress her daughter was making with her vocabulary.

"I'm sure she's doing fantastically." Angelica had to interrupt the tirade. "If she's anything like her siblings then she'll do absolutely brilliantly."

Chloe smiled proudly.

"Tim is such a whiz at his lessons." She had to practically spit the words out. "Such a favourite with his teachers." It's just a pity he tried to exorcise my grandfather's spirit to a prison on the other side, she exclaimed silently.

"I have had good reports." Chloe agreed. "It's why he's been allowed to have his friends over to stay for the holiday."

Angelica nodded politely. Over the other woman's shoulder Lettenby materialised holding his eye. He grimaced. Moaning, he rubbed at his head. Grumbling. Why on earth was he holding his eye? "What a total lot of nonsense."

"I believe in rewarding good behaviour." She continued oblivious to the extra pair of ears listening behind her. "It is so important to encourage children to do well."

"You fool." He spat at Chloe's neck. "Your children are revolting wild animals who side with the enemy. Traitors to the Elder Wood name."

Angelica kept focused on Mrs Bloom, listening to her grandfather's view. So engrossed that it took Chloe a long time to announce that she had stopped speaking.

"Oh sorry." Angelica blinked. "I'm a terrible dreamer. Not that what you were telling me wasn't interesting. I always find our little chats enlightening. You are very wise."

"Really." Chloe fanned herself with her hand to stop the slow blush crawling up her cheeks. Being told by one of the best head teachers in England that she was wise when it came to children was praise indeed. "Well I... just pick it up as I go along. Of course we did have incredibly strict parents ourselves; instilled a lot of good principles into us. I can't really boast the same for my sister. Pandora's always been a bit of a wild card."

"Pandora." Angelica nodded finding it hard to even say the alternative woman's name. If her grandfather was finding Chloe's child skills hard to stomach, he would probably suffer indigestion at the idea of Pandora's. The woman was an utter waste of time. Believing in the merits of nourishing and loving. Really. She was half the reason she came to Elder Wood. Realising that a school such as E W, a school which had upheld her grandfather's name, could not prosper under lineal managing.

Children were unruly little people who needed to be civilised. Respect was not a two way street with them. They earned it and gave it out. She did not understand why anyone would weaken to a child's demands. Everything had a place in her mind and children were firmly put to the back.

"Sorry." Chloe Bloom was talking. Vying to catch her attention. "Was there something you wanted me for?"

"Oh yes." Angelica remembered her hastily prepared plan. "I've prepared a little outing for you all. A little thank you for giving me the job."

"There's no need for that." Chloe turned an attractive shade of red again. "You have been a wonder for us all."

"Nonsense." Oh she sounded so like her

grandfather when she said that. It gave her a little thrill. If she could emanate his control she would be a happy woman indeed. "I want to show my thanks. Really. Please say Mr Bloom and yourself will join me for a drink. I have simply imagined this moment for ages, an evening where I can show my gratitude."

Expressions of joy and puzzlement mixed on Chloe's face.

"I've planned this night for a long time." She carried on quickly; she could compete for an Oscar at this rate. "Please come."

"It's a simply lovely idea." Mrs Bloom flinched as Lettenby pinched her, turning to look over her shoulder in wonder, then back. "When?"

"Oh tonight." She enthused. "It has to be."

"Well." Chloe shrugged. "We have nothing on, but the children.."

"I can organise a babysitter." Angelica offered sweetly. Inside she was delirious, her plan was almost there.

"Well all right." Once the nitty gritty place and time had been sorted, she walked back down the hall. "Maybe Pandora's right. Just maybe. Elder Wood is haunted." The words were meant to be a joke but they had far more truth in them than she ever realised.

The night proceeded at a fast rate and before anyone knew, Mr and Mrs Bloom were being bundled into a taxi by an energetic Angelica. "Come on." She told them. "We have a booking for seven."

"I must say." Farley muttered as they took a seat in the roomy cab. "This is terribly good of you Angelica."

"Not at all." The headmistress smiled at them

both, a glint sparking away in her eyes that neither noticed. "This is going to be a fabulous night. Something I have been planning for a very long time."

10

Lost Soul

The children walked up the blue hallway; icy tentacles tingling up their spines. "So Angelica..." Charlotte, who had met up with them in the library, was now informing all three. "Is and was a major part of Lettenby's plan to take over. What better idea than using a living breathing relative to help take control."

"I just can't believe it." Tim was saying, still suffering from acute shock.

"I always knew there was something odd about that woman." Christian added. "She was surely always a card short of a full deck."

Both Justin and Tim exchanged a look of amusement. No one could say that Christian had not picked up modern phrases. That specific one Tim knew his friend had borrowed from his father.

"This has to be the most unlucky school in England. Two evil head teachers in a row." Justin mused. "It's just not on."

"Three if you count that near miss with Mr

Fitzgerry." Christian remembered the gentleman with revulsion. There was a temporary period where Elder Wood was looking for candidates and he was a very appealing choice, well for Mr Bloom anyway. His sense of organisation appealed to him.

"Yes." Charlotte shuddered at the thought.

Their conversation was quick to flick back to the revelation of Angelica Dreyford. "I never expected to find out Lettenby had any living relatives to carry on the family cruel streak."

"I always expect the unexpected." Christian summed up, with a resolute sigh. "Especially with Lettenby."

"Good." The heavy sounding voice made them all jump. "That will help prepare you for what I have in store."

Christian stood firm in front of his friends, his eyes burning. "We are prepared."

"Wonderful." The head curled his lips in an unattractive way. "Then follow me."

The four children gazed at each other before taking a deep breath and putting a foot forward.

Mrs Bloom felt a little anxious as they rode through the High Street, or the closest thing the village shoppers had to it. "Are you sure Pandora will be ok with the children?" She asked.

"Of course." Angelica smiled. "She will be fine."

A few miles back at Elder Wood someone lay on the basement floor. The paint tin which had whacked her on the head lay tipped up beside her body. A trickle of blood streamed from beneath Pandora's hair-line pooling by the side of her head.

Charlotte struggled to cope with the horrific sight in front of her. Lettenby's rotten chuckle infiltrated the oxygen-starved room as his shadowy form rose. "Why?"

"Because I can." The man spoke quietly but with a tone of power. "I will regain control of this school and all the inhabitants in it."

"But why split us up?"

"Far more fun." He laughed heartily. "If you scream a little before you die."

Charlotte's eyes widened.

For a moment she felt her panic overtake her. A torturous sense started to tingle through her body. A churning had worked it's way through her stomach, before she heard Christian's final words clearly in her head. "Don't show him your fear."

"You can't do anything to me." She tried to sound brave. "Nothing."

"Can." He chanted. "I can do all sorts of things."

He lifted his arms and shut his eyes tightly just as Charlotte gasped. "Does the sight upset you my dear?"

Shaking her head, she felt too numb to talk. Never after all the years she had had of seeing ghosts had she ever seen anything like it before. It was hard to distinguish shapes in the mystical colours that were sparking from his hands. "You see I have become a little stronger. All those times that those pesky friends of yours kept sending me away, I used that time wisely, I learnt a lot."

Charlotte sat with her back to the wall, her hands trembling slightly. It was all very well to pretend you weren't scared but inside where she knew it counted, her heart was pounding away. Lettenby certainly looked a lot stronger.

"I'm glad you chose to give up." He echoed, a flash of light aiming in her direction as he pointed; the angle directly on her face. "It gave me a thrill to know that I had won. However now I fancy a bit of challenge, a game to get my kicks. So how about I let you fight me."

"Fight?" Charlotte didn't understand. "You want a battle?"

"Yes."

"Ok." Remembering the fevered chat she had earlier she agreed.

Where were Christian and the others? She wondered briefly about what Lettenby had done to them but as quick as a shot he had motioned to her to stand.

She did as she was told.

"Keep him thinking he's won". The words went round in her head. The first bolt of light shot over her head, missing her entirely. "I'll take that as a gift." She cried before she ran at the ghostly shape determined to side step any sudden moves. Those flashes looked lethal. It was all well and good for her to let him think he had won but if she didn't fight at all he would get suspicious.

Dodging light flashes like speeding bullets, Charlotte ducked just as a blue fireball hit her arm.

Tim rattled the door handle furiously. This was ridiculous. The plan they had all tried so hard to put together would fall apart if they didn't stick together. Lettenby had obviously thought what plan of action would hurt them most. Even sitting on his bed, Tim could not help but think of what was happening to his friends. The headmaster had not been known for saving souls when he was in control of Elder Wood. He was hardly in a better mood now. In fact he was worse. Burning with a deep-rooted desire for revenge.

Christian struggled to free himself from his binds. It was not easy. The red glow that had surrounded his sister was now firmly burning around him. His only hope was that if he had the light imprisoning him maybe his sister's punishment would lift. It was a vain hope. Futile in the face of such evil. Still he had to fight.

Lettenby gazed at the little girl's body as she lay on the hard ground. That would be the second victory of the day. Slowly he would get rid of all the useless enemies in his way.

Elder Wood 1842

The time ticked slowly, second by second eking out the torment of the locked away children. It was 1842 and the pupils of Elder Wood were suffering one more time at the hands of their evil Lord Lettenby. Grim faces regarded the blackboard. Children and teachers alike were all preserved in the stagnant atmosphere.

The headmaster paraded through the hall, his black

cloak swishing in his wake. His scowl etched into his features. A lifetime of achieving exactly what he wanted had taught him that his word was law. He thrived upon the thrills being in control gave him. Heavy thudded footsteps signalled his arrival as one at a time each class fell ominously silent. Who was he going to choose? The question hung precariously in the air. No one wanted him to select their room. His presence was doomed, a sign of terrors feared by many.

He stopped... he listened out in the hall, turned and entered one of the rooms. Children made gasps as they saw his black figure their fate was in his hands. Teachers glanced away as he watches the class. The day's lessons were unspoken on the pupils' lips. Lettenby surveyed his charges. Coughed sharply and then meticulously selected the unfortunate soul who was going to receive his wrath for the day. An example to the rest of the runny nosed little boys who were under his control. All those parents filled with hopes about the good work he would be doing with their heirs. All that lovely money. Oh he was going to lick them into shape all right.

He picked one boy, a red haired young pupil with a history of embarrassing activities to his name. The runt of the litter. Lettenby remembered him well. On interview day wasn't he the child who was attached to his mother? The freckled, disgusting brat who had cowered at his desk? Well he would soon sort him out. Calling him to the side and regarding his ink stained hands he smirked triumphantly. Ah twenty canes should sort that. He would not repeat that mistake. Not whilst he was alive.

As he parted his unmistakable black cloak, he revealed the slightest glimpse of his grotesque etched cane. Twelve mouths grimaced and twelve pairs of eyes widened. Ordering the teacher to open the door louder, there was a *use in letting all the pupils hear his punishment. It made them fear him even more. As he brought the oak wood stick down on the white sweaty palm a sole scream echoed across the hall and throughout the school.*

Elder Wood 2010

Back in the present the same oppressed atmosphere filled the air. Screams of pain swept through the school. Wolfgang sniffed the blackness curiously. Something was up.

That sweet sickly smell of danger. Chalky smoke rose from the blackboards in the empty classrooms. Elder Wood was transforming for its final battle.

The newly painted rooms started to swirl faster and faster. Desks, brand new, changed shape and then colour. Benches appeared.

Lettenby threw back his head and laughed. Christian Cortex looked up at him from beneath veiled lashes. A look of bravery was clearly etched into his features.

The second had finally arrived and Lettenby promised himself that he was going to enjoy every minute ticking by off the clock. Christian was finally going to succumb to his wiles. He had been tough but finally Lettenby had the chance to break him.

Without flinching, Christian kept his eyes homed in on Lettenby. If he thought this was it, then he was seriously mistaken.

Tim sat up. He had been frustratingly cooped up in his room for the last hour. Finally lying on his bed, he had decided to try to relax. At least for as long as possible.

A while ago he had heard Lettenby's ghostly footsteps walking down the hall. It had driven him half-mad trying to figure out which of his friends he was picking off the list next. He had sat motionless, scarcely able to breathe as he tried to listen for clues. When he heard nothing. Nothing but his own soft breaths. He knew that his fears were going to turn to himself.

Was he next?

When would Lettenby come for him?

It was a terrible ordeal. Tim found that his life was becoming weirder by the week. Who would believe that he was being kept hostage in his own home by a spirit?

That was when he had chosen to get on his bed. At that point he was positive that Lettenby would come bursting in on him at any moment. That had been a good twenty minutes ago.

As he sat on his mattress he heard that noise again. Scratch. There was a noise outside his room. Getting to his feet, he listened. His ear pressed against the door.

"Tim!"

"Louise?"

"Yes."

He stood back. "How on earth did you get out?"

"I can't explain." She hissed.

"Why?"

"You won't believe it." She whispered. "Anyway you'll see soon enough for yourself. We have to get you out."

"We?" He asked. "Is Kim with you?"

"Not exactly."

Frowning he tried to make up his mind what was going on outside. Very strange occurrences which were getting more odd by the second.

"Stand back." His sister ordered. "We're breaking in."

"Ok." His voice was slightly wobbly.

Doing what his sister told him, he stared in open-mouthed wonder as the first speckle of sparkle shot through his keyhole. Each tiny dot shimmered like the effect of a sparkler on Bonfire Night. Tim did not know what they were. Whatever, Louise trusted it. Stranger things had happened.

Tim stood back against the bed as the particles of energy poured through the hole. Getting faster and fuller. As they started to shimmy on the other side they pulled into shape. The dots all joined together like one huge dot-to- dot puzzle. Tim tried to make out what was happening. It appeared to be a materialisation. The same as when Christian would pop up in front of him.

As the lights joined together they shone. So brightly he had to close his eyes against the strength. Like a thousand night stars pulling on each other's strength. He found himself thinking about who it could be. Was it one of his old friends, the professor? The elder of the spirit world.

Opening his eyes he gasped.

Suki trailed the scent. Wolfgang pawed after her in his usual loveable fashion. There was something going to happen. He had felt it the first occasion. That strange whiff of something special. When the children had believed it to be safe, he had been one of the first to pick up on the scent of a showdown. This was different. This time he could feel the scent was much stronger. Whatever was going to come their way, was going to be the final battle.

He padded up to the open door Suki had found was the best access they had. That evil woman had thought that by barring them from the house they would remain imprisoned. Ha! She didn't know how intelligent they were.

Suki struggled to ease her way in. Those extra pounds she had put on were making life tough. Wolfgang still adored her whatever shape or size she was and thought she was the most beautiful thing alive. He followed her into the hall and froze. Suki had let out the most awful whine.

Tim blinked once. "Uh hello."

In front stood an ex-pupil of the Elder Wood school. After hearing so many stories of Christian's friends, this was the first time he was actually coming face to face with one of them.

"Hello." The boy spoke faintly and with a serious air. "We need to go."

"Right, fine." Tim looked at the door. "How?"

"Like this." With a look of concentration, he closed his eyes.

Bam!

The door rattled. The handle turned and the door flung open.

"Wow." Tim breathed. "Thank you."

A thought struck him just as they were walking out onto the landing. "Sorry." He didn't want what he was about to actually suggest to sound at all ungrateful in any way. "But couldn't you just have done that door thing from the other side."

"Yes." The boy said, after a moment of silence, leaving Timothy puzzled. Two seconds passed before he uttered the next few syllables. "But my way is much more fun. Don't you think?"

Tim smiled and nodded his agreement. It was a relief to know Christian's friends were as interesting as he was.

"Let's go." The boy led the way.

Louise was waiting for him up the hall. "Isn't it great?" She enthused when she saw her brother. "The boys have come to save us."

"Great." He agreed falling into step beside her and after a moment's hesitation. Battling with the ghosts of the world did knock you for six. "Boys?"

"The pupils." She looked at him as if to say he was the most stupid person on the planet. "The old pupils of Elder Wood."

"Christian's friends?" He was shocked. "All of them."

"Yep." She smiled. "I think it is marvellous. Just when you think there's no hope, our saviours rush in to save the day and they're so cute."

"They?" Tim wasn't sure he could sustain a lot more of these type of shocks. And cute? The last time he checked, his little sister was way too young to find boys cute. Disgusting maybe.

"Yes." She rolled her eyes. "The rest of them. What did you think? That Benjamin would come all on his own? They've come to defeat Lettenby. We need a type of army."

"Brilliant." He eyed the back of the slightly taller boy with interest. So these were Christian's school buddies. In that fleeting second he had all the trust in the world in them.

The boy took them to a staircase at the end of the hall. "We're going to the attic." Tim looked at the boy for some sort of clue. He wasn't asking to know the whole plan, but the odd hint would be good. It wasn't too much to ask really. He guessed they could either have some serious tricks in mind or they would go in there and physically take their revenge. Personally he hoped for the last one despite his warnings to his little sisters.

"We're going to rescue the girl."

"Charlotte?" Tim battled to keep himself from flying up the stairs. "Is she hurt?"

"Yes." The boy remained focused.

'You can't just say yes!' Tim wanted to yell. Scream, I need a few more details than that. He wanted to ask all the questions he wanted to know but he knew it would do no good. The spirit was too out of this realm. He was far different to the friendly Christian he was so familiar chatting with.

Not wasting a moment of time, the three walked up the steps. The attic door was shut tight with the same kind of glowing lock that signified the evil head and his ways. Within a second the ghost had broken the red glow and the door burst open.

"Charlotte!" Tim stumbled up the stairs. "Speak to me. It's Timothy."

A murmur attracted his attention from the side of the room and he ran straight to her. "Charlotte." He crouched beside her helping her up. "Are you all right?"

"Kind of." She rubbed her arm. It still hurt but it was nothing she feared compared to what Christian was probably suffering.

"Is he still here?" Tim looked round frantically.

"No."

Timothy and Charlotte made their way down to the others. Louise ran to her and hugged her with joy. "You're ok." She squeezed her hard.

"Ow." Charlotte flinched as the little girl caught her arm.

"Sorry." Louise was too excited to be too apologetic. "Have you heard about what's happened? Has Tim told you about Christian's friends?"

"No." She brushed the strands of hair out of her eyes. Her encounter with Lettenby had left her in a slightly messy state. "Oh." Noticing the boy for the first time, she jumped.

The boy nodded at her. Without further ado he started to lead them back down the hall. "We must hurry." He afforded them the odd word. "The lady is hurt. Time is of the essence."

Charlotte wiggled her eyebrows at Timothy over Louise's head. "The lady?"

"There's no point asking." Tim answered quietly. "They are boys of few words. He is just focused on getting to Lettenby."

Charlotte tried to keep control of her fears whilst they made their way to the basement. Lady? That had to be Pandora.

At the top of the stairs Benjamin waited patiently. A cluster of sparkles shone and transformed into a group of boys a similar age to Ben. They seemed to talk through telepathy, faces serious.

"We will go now."

"But Pandora?" Charlotte was shocked.

"She will be fine." One of the older boys replied. "Time is running out."

Tim knew that the tone of urgency in his voice was

141

valid. The boys probably had enough time to sort Lettenby out and leave. They didn't want to waste time.

Lettenby closed his eyes and released Christian from his red prison. He took a moment before he brought the cane down hard. His eyes sparkled with the pleasure of knowing that it would make sickening contact with his bone. He felt the swoop of the wood the length of his aim but at the final moment there was no thud.

Snapping his eyes open he growled. "Boy!" He roared. "What are you doing?"

"Fighting." He had caught and was clenching on to the vicious tool. "Did you really think we gave up? Never."

Lettenby struggled to release the weapon, physically tugging. "You little fool." He spat. "This will only prolong your agony. You can't fight me alone."

Christian yanked the cane but Lettenby was physically powerful, far stronger. What he needed was a diversionary tactic, something to attract his attention.

"He is not alone."

The words rang out in the air. Yes that will do it, Christian thought. The headmaster turned around, his eyes raking over the scene. Christian found that he now had control of the stick. He stood triumphantly with it in hand.

"NO." The cry was so anguished it was painful. "You can not be here. I took care of you."

"Our friend is never alone." Benjamin was the voice of the group. "Christian is a good soul, a person who was strong and kind in life. A spirit who is now rewarded with something you can never have."

"What?"

"Freedom." Ben carried on. "Christian can be here because he wants to be. He has made ties with people who draw him, want him near. You however have no such friends and are being called back to the spirit world. Somewhere you won't return from."

"Rubbish." He cried.

Benjamin looked serious.

"Who is going to make me? Two boys? Weak children?" He laughed.

Until he saw something which stopped his laughter forever.

Elder Wood's pupils materialised through the wall. Rows of grim faces all relentless in their movement forward. All looking as lust-thirsty for revenge as Lettenby. "You can not." His voice actually shook. "You can not be here."

"Uh." Mr Corbett, one of the maths teachers of the day coughed. "I beg to differ Sir. Oh hang on, I do not need to call you that any longer. Lord Lettenby. We have every right to be here. You however are lingering where you have no business. This is no longer your school. You have no control over the inhabitants of this building and you can hurt no one any more."

Eagle Eyes digested this piece of news with a lot of discomfort. His face turned an attractive puce, furiously becoming deeper in colour until it looked as if he had turned brown. "This is an absolute atrocity. I demand to be given the right to roam around my own school."

"You do not seem to understand." The maths teacher indulged him in one more explanation. This time far simpler. "You have no place here." He took a breath before delivering the final blow. "Oh you have a message."

"From who?" Suddenly Lettenby reacted as if he had been punched in the stomach, backing away hastily. "Hang on. I don't want a message."

"Tough." Mr Corbett actually smiled. "You're going to get one."

All the pupils took a step forward as Mr Corbett started to speak. "This message comes to you from The Professor."

"The elder of the spirit world?" Lettenby's voice shook, his hands raised as if to shield him. He couldn't get over so many hate filled eyes staring at him, baying for his blood. The years of torment were over. The victims had claimed their right to stand up to the persecutor who had hurt them for so many years.

"I forget." Mr Corbett winked at Christian while he pretended to think. "How did it go? Oh yes, it went like this."

Within a minute the words which sprouted from his mouth had Lettenby screaming. "No!"

All the pupils joined in. Chanting louder. The words sparked off a misty coil, one reminiscent of the white smoke that belonged to the spirit world. It circled Lettenby's form, enshrouding him like the red energy he had used on many before. Only this barricade was much stronger than any fire Lettenby could create. The mist rose up. It was a prison of justice, something he just could not break out of.

Bang. Sparks flew just as Charlotte and the others stumbled into the room. The scene was quite amazing. One of such absolute magnitude that children who had not had experience in spiritual matters would have found difficult. Timothy had not witnessed so many ghosts in one room.

Charlotte was regarding the scene with an expression of understanding. The children who had been so wronged. The original pupils of Elder Wood had come for redemption. It was an interesting sight to see so many faces. The pupils who had learnt in this building so many years ago. She fell quiet. Happy just to witness the fight when she heard a familiar call. "Lottie?"

Jumping, she saw her older brother heading up the stairs. "Where were you?" He was grumbling. "I told you I did not want to come up here. This place is majorly creeping me out. Did you know that there were these weird sparks of light following me up the hall. I think the electricity in this place is faulty or something."

Oh. No. Charlotte turned to see that the scene was unfolding without interruption. Rushing up to him she tried to stop him. "Callum. You shouldn't have come. I'll be down in a minute. Wait for me at the door."

"Who do you think I am? Your servant."

"No." She grabbed his arm, trying to pull him back through to the stars. "Please Callum go downstairs."

"Hey what is going on in there?"

The chanting in the classroom was getting louder. Surely her brother couldn't hear? He had never seen ghosts. Never even shown a hint that he had the same gift. Why was he heading towards the classroom in that freaky way?

"Callum." She tried to explain. "It's nothing."

It was too late. Hoping he wouldn't see it, she accompanied him to the door, trying to look normal. Well as normal as possible when you had knowledge that a demonic headmaster in the room in front of you was actually being exorcised. He had made it to the doorway and was standing there with a look of shock etched all over his face. Her answer.

Lettenby who had been rather stunned himself by the onslaught of so many familiar faces took one look at Callum's strange get up. What was the name of it? Out of the ordinary clothes.

Christian who was still clutching the cane, the tool of so much misery, gawped unashamedly as the cause of so much destruction met his long fate. His long overdue date with destiny.

The headmaster once feared by so many started to shake as he span in the swirly mist. He knew that where he was heading, no one could bring him back. His body started to disappear. His eagle eyes were the final traces of his evil presence, staring at Christian helplessly. For once he had not an angry look but a cowardly one, his eyes connected with the boy. Blinking as they started to fade, to leave the world forever. In those final moments they both knew that they would never see each other again. Christian and Lord Lettenby belonged to different worlds. The boy would always be allowed to travel betwixt the worlds. The evil headmaster would be sent to the place where he could absolutely never come back from.

In the final moments Christian felt a rush of emotion. Gazing into the eyes of such a cruel heart. "Chris!"

The familiar echo had him look back. There was Timothy and the rest of his friends waiting at the door. His support.

Turning back, the cane was brought down hard

over his knee. With a loud thwack he snapped the implement in two. The two eyes closed and were gone.

The second that his soul was enraptured the whole building shook. Christian closed his eyes against the strength of the mini earthquake and when he opened his eyes he was rewarded with the sight of his little sister. Free of her binds.

"Sarah!" He cried hurrying to her.

11

The End of an Era

Charlotte dropped Tim's hand, which had quietly slipped into hers just when the mayhem had reached a penultimate moment. "Is he ok?"

"I think he's probably a bit mystified." Tim replied looking at a pale and trembling version of Charlotte's sibling.

"Not Callum." She pointed at who she meant. "Christian."

"Oh." He focused his attention on him. "I hope so."

"I think maybe you should talk to him." She encouraged, gently shoving him forward. "Remind him you're friends."

Tim walked forward and waited patiently whilst he said goodbye to his past friends.

Chris had left Sarah to recover at one of the desks. He hadn't been able to talk to Benjamin for years and years. Being able to see him again was miraculous.

He found saying goodbye very difficult. "I can not understand how you knew." He exclaimed. "About Lettenby. How you came when I most needed you."

"That's what friends are for." Ben smiled. "You stuck up for us all the first time. We couldn't let you fight Lettenby for the final time without help. Not on your own."

"Have you been watching him?" Christian wanted to know.

"We knew he had been up to a few antics. The spirit council has been wanting to catch him for a while. Up to now you seemed to be handling him. You and your friends."

Christian felt his eyes swivel to Timothy. His friend was smiling encouragingly. "Yes we make a good team."

"We have to go." Ben looked down at his feet. "We want to make sure that Lettenby is given the worst punishment by the court."

"I'd love to come." Christian enthused then felt a pang of fear. "Though maybe I've had enough contact with that soul."

"Glad to hear it." He grinned. "I'll see you."

"See you."

The maths teacher made his way over to collect the boys. "I expect you thought The Professor had forgotten about you." He winked at Christian. "Never. He will now see that Lettenby never ever sets foot on Elder Wood soil again. We will make sure of that."

The children gazed enraptured as the boys started to disappear. Sparkles of colour mystically spiralling before them. The spirits were on their way to a higher plane.

Timothy slapped Christian on the shoulder. "Everything can go back to normal now."

"As normal as possible." Christian agreed.

"Look." Tim sighed taking him aside. "I know that the situation has been a bit weird with us. I just... lately so many things have happened."

"I know."

"I've been keeping a secret." Tim confessed. "I think I know how Lettenby came back. Meg had taken a couple of his cufflinks. Possessions which could have brought him back."

Christian stared at him in amazement. "Why didn't you tell me?"

"Because." He looked at him. "I wanted the problem to go away, I thought if I kept it quiet..."

"Tim." Chris reached out and clutched his shoulder. Not in an angry way but with a sense of reassurance. "We're friends. You should tell me about anything that is worrying you. Anyway I doubt it was the only reason he was drawn back. Lettenby would have found a way. At least now we know wherever he's gone, he has gone for good."

Tim smiled at his friend; he was so understanding, far more sensitive of nature than he could ever be. He was proud to have earned his friendship. A friendship he would never throw away.

"If I am going to be truthful. There's something." He decided to be honest. If anything had been learnt by this experience it was that he had to trust his friend, tell the truth. "A something I feel has been building up some problems. I have been feeling... "

"I know." He smiled. "It's Charlotte isn't it?"

"What?" Tim's cheeks felt like they were on fire.

"I worked it out." He was quite relieved as he stated. "It is not our friendship. You have started to like her."

"I…"

"That is it. I know it is." He spoke with conviction.

"Ok." He admitted letting Charlotte catch his eye and smiled happily. Black hair prettily swinging behind her as she helped her brother sit down. The usually in charge Callum looked about ready to pass out. Well, seeing a ghostly exorcising it was a little out of the ordinary. He would never be the same again.

"I do like her." He found himself uttering the words without thinking. "She understands me."

"Good." Christian smiled. "I think she's great for a girl. Most go all strange if they feel a chill around them, shriek and make such a fuss if they catch a glimpse of ghosts but she is so calm about it all."

"Exactly." Tim agreed, feeling like he was really talking to his friend again. "I think she's radical."

Christian was so pleased, a smile by the likes that Tim had not seen on him in a long long time.

Tim prepared himself to ask the question. He didn't exactly pleasure the thought but if he didn't he knew that they would never have the same friendship again. "I thought maybe you liked her too."

"I do." He admitted before seeing his point. "But not like that. I have a little secret of my own."

"You do?" Tim narrowed his eyes in wonder.

"Yep."

"You've met a girl."

"Kind of." He was blushing.

Tim was amazed. "Is she..?"

"Oh yes." He elaborated. "I met her at a spirit party. She's my age and we like the same things. I'd love you to meet her."

"I would love to." He couldn't wait to tell Charlotte.

"What girl?" Sarah asked as she ambled over. "That one I saw you with outside the house."

Christian groaned. "Were you spying on me?"

"No." She looked away. "Kind of."

"Well yes." He sighed. "If you have to know, she is the very same."

"Oh." She looked back at him. "I like her."

"How do you know her?"

"She popped over to the house the other day?"

"Really?"

"Asking about you." His little sister carried on. "Are you in love?"

"Sarah." He groaned. "I'm only twelve."

"Still." She smiled. "It could be."

Charlotte winked at Tim. They were both watching the brother and sister reunite. "So that has taken care of that." She looked up at Tim and watched as he took her hand, just a slight movement between themselves but one which filled her with an unexplainable joy. Together she knew that Christian, Tim and herself would always be friends.

"That's it." He agreed with much relief and a great big grin as she squeezed his hand in return. "Elder Wood is now totally free."

12

The Future

The Blooms returned late that night. The minute Chloe entered the hall she sighed at the much-improved atmosphere. "Oh that's better. The heating is back on."

"What?" Angelica was on alert, her eyes darting from one side of the room to another as she frantically tried to discover what had happened.

"That cold feeling. It's gone."

"Oh." Looking round her face turned grim. Alexander? Something was wrong.

Rushing off, she left Mr and Mrs Bloom staring after her in wonder.

"Little highly strung isn't she?" Farley announced in an unamused tone. "Couldn't keep still all through the evening, almost like she couldn't wait to get back here."

"Try not to take it personally." Reaching up Chloe kissed him lightly on the cheek. "All great thinkers are a little eccentric. It happens to the best of us."

Shrugging the matter off he let his wife lead him to bed.

Searching the ground floor, Mrs Dreyford was more than aggrieved to find no trace of her relative. The energy which pulsated around her normally so fiercely had died down to nothing and she found herself reluctantly facing the fact that her Alexander had gone. He had finally left Elder Wood.

A faint whimpering caught her attention as she silently fumed, a tiny annoying cluster of shrieks. Angrily she stalked down the corridor and flung open the door to the library to see a scene that drove home the final blow. Even her dog had betrayed her and with that awful excuse for a dog. That utterly disgusting Wolfgang and her dog Suki were curled up together nestling between them a lively litter of wriggling bodies. Oh how ridiculous! Turning on her heel Angelica, still seething, slammed her way out.

The children had fun watching the fireworks go off. Unbeknown to them a surprise was taking place in the library, a far sweeter one and one which was going to provide them all with a good and long awaited reason to celebrate. All that night the new headmistress acted strangely, mumbling about knowing she should not have left everything up to him. "It's all gone wrong." She could be heard screeching at ear piecing levels. "Years I've put into this and now it's all ruined." Without Alexander by her side she knew that she would not be able to carry out her strict regime. He was the main engine behind her plan, the fuel of a masterpiece she was physically giving shape to and now it was all over.

Mr and Mrs Bloom could not understand it. Overnight their calm and collected headmistress had turned into a total nightmare. Fraught, talking to herself, walking in and out of rooms at a rate of knots.

The next morning her letter of resignation was left on the study table. Mysteriously she disappeared over night. A note was left claiming that she simply had to go away on urgent business and considering the current situation, giving Suki and the puppies over to the Bloom family.

Pandora, who had suffered a fairly bad but not too serious head injury, stayed in bed the next day claiming that she had fallen down the stairs. It was a plausible excuse and one that Chloe put down yet again to her infernal clumsiness. Pandora didn't mind, though she was upset that the children had not told her about Lettenby's return. She was too glad about his departure to make too much fuss and spent her time instead getting better as quickly as she could, for she could not let the new head of Elder Wood be chosen without her opinion being considered.

The Education Board were considering the post for new head and were submitting candidates as quickly as possible in preparation for the continuation of the school term. Charlotte came to visit as much as her mother would allow during the rest of the holidays. When she found out about the puppies there was nothing anyone could do to keep her indoors.

"Mum is going to make sure the next candidate is better suited to Elder Wood." Tim had told her at the front of the much happier feeling building.

"Will the Education board let her interfere with their decision?"

Obviously Charlotte didn't know his mum as well

157

as he did. "You try stopping her." He laughed. "She even admitted that she may consider someone a little less strict, said there may be something to be learnt from Aunt Pandora's laid back attitude." He put on a very amusing version of his mother's voice, having overheard her talking to his father that very day. "Apparently the highly stressed people are always the first to crack."

Charlotte giggled.

"Aunt Pandora's going to be far more involved with the influence over the new candidate. That way we can make sure that the new head has no evil ties."

"Good." Charlotte smiled hopping from foot to foot. "Now please can we go and see the puppies."

"Uh huh." Tim who himself couldn't get enough time with the new arrivals due to the incredibly long line of visitors desperate to see the new family each day.

Leading the way, they met up with the rest of the gang all heading for the library, the most popular meeting place in recent days. The children all tumbled into the den in a frenzy of delight. Wolfgang, the proud father rose up to let the children take a peek at his suckling brood. He was looking as healthy as ever, his eyes were sparkling and if it was at all possible Timothy was sure he could see him smiling. Suki, proudly showing her brood off, was all too keen for the faces to crowd around her. Seven tiny heads all lapping up their quota of milk wriggled into their mother's warm fur.

"Aw they're adorable." Charlotte knelt next to the tiny wiggling pups, exchanging a warm smile with Tim. The girls, Louise and Kim were as close as humanly possible to the little bundles of joy. They gently stroked the top of the smallest puppy's head watching as Suki carefully propped him back in place with her snout. Justin, standing behind them, watched with a wrapped expression as one tiny pup squeaked with the straining effort of climbing up his mother's side. After a mountainous climb he was amply rewarded with a fresh supply of milk.

All pairs of eyes gazed on as another pup, eager for his fair share, wriggled close but, with astonishing speed and a cry, lost his footing and tumbled back down into the blanketed basket. The puppies were better than any form of entertainment and were the main attraction for the whole household. They were, even after a few days, regular members of the family, securely having found a place in the hearts of the whole family. The whole litter were still getting to grips with the strange idea of balance and regularly had to be put back into their baskets after a sleepy exploration landed them on the floor. Louise, Suki's new helper, was very eager to re-attach the pup to his mother.

Patting Wolfgang gently, Christian had flicked a quick content look at his own friend Poppy, who was gazing adoringly at the loving happy family. Poppy with her coppery locks and blue green eyes was now a regular face among the crowd.

"They look so happy." Christian whispered, not wanting to disturb the Christmas card scene.

"They are." Tim agreed. "They represent the new generation at Elder Wood."

The End